Getting Serious

D1086279

Also by Gordon Weaver

Count a Lonely Cadence
The Entombed Man of Thule
Such Waltzing Was Not Easy
Give Him a Stone
Circling Byzantium

Getting Serious

Stories by Gordon Weaver

Louisiana State University Press
Baton Rouge and London 1980

Design: Joanna Hill
Typeface: Baskerville
Composition: G&S Typesetters, Inc.

The stories in this volume appeared, in slightly different form, in *Iowa Review*, *Southern Review*, *Quarterly West*, *Ploughshares*, and *Antioch Review*. "Getting Serious" was first published in *Sewanee Review*, LXXXV (Fall, 1977). Copyright 1977 by the University of the South. Reprinted by permission of the editor.

Library of Congress Cataloging in Publication Data

Weaver, Gordon.
    Getting serious.

    CONTENTS: The Engstrom girls.—Hog's heart.—Macklin's epigraphic loss.
[etc.]
    I. Title.
PZ4.W3628Ge   [PS3573.E17]   813'.54   80-17737
ISBN 0-8071-0777-8
ISBN 0-8071-0778-6 (pbk.)

Second Printing (April, 1981)

For Judy, Kristina, Anna, Jessica—
and for Thomas Reiter, the poet

Contents

The Engstrom Girls   1

Hog's Heart   13

Macklin's Epigraphic Loss   31

If a Man Truly in His Heart   61

The Cold   79

Getting Serious   97

"I can promise to say nothing that is untrue, but do not think I shall want to say all; and I reserve the right to lie by omission. Unless I change my mind."

Giuseppe di Lampedusa, *Places of My Infancy*

The Engstrom Girls

I am something, know I am that something, then become something else. Does this mean I lose what I have been? I hope to prove otherwise.

I accept all, knowing I am caught, paralyzed in the process that diminishes my future each day, while, in the same breath, it steals my past. If I'm lucky I might live to be as old as Grandma Sorenson, who was ninety-four when I saw her, the year I was twelve and went to Hambro, Illinois, with my aunts and my mother, the Engstrom girls.

Of course their names were not Engstrom anymore. But in Hambro, long before, they had been the Engstrom girls, just as I was the Hansen boy in my neighborhood in Milwaukee. My mother was the middle sister, Anne.

Aunt Osa was the oldest. She was ten when my mother was born, just before the turn of the century. She, along with Grandma Sorenson, kept house for the family in Hambro after my real grandmother, Grandmother Engstrom, died in 1907. The dates are in a huge clasped Bible brought from Sweden in my grandmother's steamer box in 1883. It is in Swedish, but dates and names are the same in any language.

At Aunt Osa's house there were two staple pleasures, good food, the pillar upon which her home stood, and license of activity. I could get away with nearly anything there. She had had a son who died of bulbar polio one evening, sitting in their kitchen. Aunt Osa and Uncle Adolph sat with him while his constricting muscles pulled his head backwards, forcing his eyes to roll back in his head. I think now it must have been difficult for Aunt Osa to see me grow much beyond twelve, when I shot out legs and arms as long as my father's.

She only reprimanded me once. It was the year before the trip we made to Hambro. I had a rubber ball; I was baseball-happy then. Aunt Osa's husband, Adolph, who came originally from Memphis, was irritated by my avowing shortly after I arrived for a visit that my favorite baseball player was Jackie Robinson.

"Why," he asked, "can't you pick some white man for your favorite?" He had had twelve inches removed from his stomach for ulcers shortly before, so smoked only Sano cigarettes in a special holder filtered by a crystal cartridge. "Look at that Blackwell now, why can't he be your favorite?" He had intimidated me long before this by announcing that he intended to teach me manners: to say *sir* and *m'am*, to make formal introductions, to hold the chair for my aunt when we sat down for meals.

But I had the rubber ball in the house, and I started throwing it up to the ceiling of the living room and catching the rebound. "Stop that, Oskar," Aunt Osa said from the kitchen; she was cooking. I stopped for a few minutes, then started again. I was pretty sure of myself in that house.

"Will you stop that?" she called. I did, but not for long. I think I had just caught the ball, my mouth still open in surprise and suspense, when she materialized in the kitchen doorway, spoon or spatula in hand, aproned, and with a look of anger in her face that showed the strength a person derives from human loss.

"Damnit, Oskar, stop it!" she said. I didn't move for a full minute after she went back to the kitchen. It was the essence, the core of the need for order in life that rang in her voice, expressed with a despair that might have come from that long night spent watching her only child die. It paralyzed me. That kind of strength doesn't grow overnight.

Her strength could be terrible because it so seldom showed itself. It took my bratty conduct with a rubber ball in her spotless parlor to betray just a flicker of it, one more powerful than all the wailing and threats some parents use, more lasting in effect than repeated razor straps or woodsheds. That strength grew slowly in the town of Hambro.

She was past thirty when she married Uncle Adolph, who had come in the course of his travels to Hambro to operate the telegraph for the Illinois Central. From the time of her mother's death, Aunt Osa had helped raise her sisters and share the housekeeping with Grandma Sorenson, who paid more attention to my grandfather and left the children to Osa's charge.

When Osa married, Grandma Sorenson had only two things to say. Of Adolph, who was blond then, she said, "Well, he's not Swedish, but he *looks* Swedish," and she confided to my aunt once after Grandfather Engstrom had left the house to pitch horseshoes with his new son-in-law, "I'll always say this for your father, he never did go and marry again."

My Uncle Adolph had been everywhere as a telegraph operator. He was a sports fan, followed the boxing and baseball news avidly, and from the card games he taught me when I visited with them, the year of my parents' divorce, he must have been something of a gambler once too.

"Hit me," I said, praying he didn't have another face card to go with his king showing. He dealt me an ace, and I began to dream of coming in under twenty-one with five cards for a double score.

"Yes," he said, "the ship foundered, rolled over like a horse on its side, and the only ones that made it to shore were myself and a cook's helper. There were supposed to be sharks in those waters."

"Hit me," I said. A deuce. "Does Borneo have jungles?"

"Certainly it was a jungle," he said, inserting a fresh Sano in his holder. "That's what I'm coming to if you'll give me a chance. Don't interrupt a man when he's telling you something."

"Hit me again," but this time it was an eight, and I broke. I flipped my cards over and pushed them toward him.

"Hah!" he snorted. "Didn't make it, did you? Well, all we had, he had a gun, a single-action navy repeater, and I had a knife I'd had sense enough to grab in the galley before I jumped over the fantail. We started cutting through the bush hoping to find some kind of settlement. We knew the Dutch had plantations some-where around. We were going through the bush, and a snake dropped from the limb of a tree, and I heard him scream. Be-fore I could turn and help him, he was dead."

He paused and shuffled the deck. Over his shoulder I could see my aunt's lips moving as she read still another exotic cook book. I was shocked that she could sit there quietly with a book while someone who had been shipwrecked off Borneo shuffled a deck of cards in her parlor.

"Now," my Uncle Adolph said, "let's have a few hands of ca-sino. Oh, and when you want another card in blackjack, you don't have to keep saying *hit me*. Just scratch the table with your cards like this," and he showed me the gambler's motion with his hands.

My aunt said, "That was before I civilized him. Ask him to tell you about the time he came to Hambro and Mr. Frank Lind-quist, who had the first moving-picture theater there, came and asked me if I wouldn't give meals to a poor fellow who'd come from New Orleans to operate the telegraph. Why, the first day he came to the door, your grandfather came into the kitchen where Grandma Sorenson and I were fixing supper, and he said, 'Osa, there's a young fellow at the door who looks hungry and says he's to talk to you.'"

He and my aunt went on to talk of Mr. Frank Lindquist, and of Bengt Berntson, who had a very large collection of hunting guns, and of Grandma Sorenson's distrust of my uncle's lack of Swedish ancestry, and of Mrs. Swenson, who lived next door and who I knew used to give my mother pastries to eat, paper bags full of them, and of my grandfather, who died when I was less than a year old.

I see that my uncle was a hero; I see it *now*. Because he had come to town just over thirty years old then, and such a new-comer was rare when many of the young men of Hambro were going to Chicago to make wages, and he married my aunt—also over thirty—who was well on her way to being an old maid. I'm told that's not a pleasant thing to be in a small town.

"Let's go to Hambro sometime," I said, "and go to Mr. Frank Lindquist's movie."

"You'd never get your uncle there again," she said. "Do you know where he ran off to just after we were married? Ohio, to see Jack Dempsey fight Jess Willard, that's where."

"I had a job of work to telegraph that fight to New Orleans for the New Orleans *Times-Picayune*," my uncle said through his cigarette smoke. "I dropped a bundle on the big farmer that time too. I still think Jack had plaster casts on his hands. Nobody can break a man's jaw like that with his plain hands." He sounded as if he had tried.

"But let's go there sometime," I insisted.

"We'll see," Aunt Osa said.

"Play your cards," my uncle said.

When that round of lawyers and court appearances in my parents' divorce was over, I was taken back to my mother. "Be nice to your mother now," Aunt Osa told me on the train between Chicago and Milwaukee. "She's having a terrible time."

It was then, during and just after the divorce, that I noticed how often my mother looked at the pictures. I found one lying out on a table in the dining room that I had never seen before: my father in his uniform as a flying sergeant during the First World War.

"Why did they wear such funny uniforms?" I asked her after Aunt Osa had left.

"They weren't so funny if you'd seen them," she answered.

"It was the army the same as it is now, wasn't it?"

"Of course it was. You ought to talk to your cousin Thurston in Hambro sometime—" she pronounced it as Swedes do, *Torsten*—"he lost a leg because they kept him on guard duty all night in freezing cold at Fort Snelling, Minnesota. He could tell you. Some disease set in and they took his leg."

"I don't have a cousin Thurston," I said.

"Yes, you do," she said a bit harshly. "He's not really your cousin, but he's Grandma Sorenson's nephew, so he might just as well be related to you."

"I know who Grandma Sorenson is. Aunt Osa told me about

her, and once I heard you talking about her," I said. I learned during this time of the divorce to make her happy by saying something about something or someone from Hambro.

"Here," my mother said, "here's a picture of Grandma Sorenson and myself and your father and your grandfather." She said it as though she had only picked it up out of her pocket. But it meant going to the dining room and stretching to reach a large cardboard box from the top of the china cupboard. It was brimful of photographs, even a few tintypes, and many that were printed on a stiff cardboard backing that had yellowed. They were all of the Engstrom family and friends in Hambro, and, except for a few taken on later visits, they all predated 1917.

"Do you know who this is?" she asked me. We were on the sofa. The picture was oval-shaped, and held the solemn faces of three blond girls, all with white dresses on.

"You?" I guessed, trying to be shrewd.

"But which one?"

"In the middle."

"No. That's my cousin Einar. Your second cousin."

"He looks like a little girl."

"His hair wasn't cut until he was almost six years old, and I cried so the day I saw him after he'd been to the barber."

"Does he still have blond hair?"

"He doesn't have any hair anymore. But he did then. That's your Aunt Claire. See how blond we all were. Grandma Sorenson said we had the most beautiful blond hair all in one family she'd ever seen. I remember that when it was taken in Hambro. I was ten—no, I must have been eleven. My hair didn't begin to get dark until I married your father. Claire couldn't have been more than three or four." She wasn't really talking to me anymore.

She had pictures, newspaper clippings telling of births, deaths, and marriages that Grandma Sorenson mailed to her, even a scrapbook she kept in high school, in which she had laboriously recorded team cheers circa 1911–1915. Aunt Osa learned strength in thirty years in Hambro. My mother had stability there, and evenness to her life, and meaning. In Hambro, all things had been right, and they still were; she needed only to look at the pictures to be sure of it.

My father had always been a sociable man. Through contacts in the Masons he got a job selling some machine that was in some way vital to the production of other machines which in turn made munitions of some kind. I have heard my Aunt Osa sadly reflect that my father paid $40,000 in income tax in 1943. That kind of money was too much for him, and he blossomed into the kind of man who was not at all a part of the scheme of things as my mother had learned it in the Swedish community of Hambro.

She first took divorce action in 1945, when she learned my father was keeping a woman in St. Paul, where he often traveled, and had even taken her with him on some business trips. My brothers were in the service and my sister was already married. She took less alimony than she could have gotten and went to live with the photographs from the time that had always had a sense, a logic and a meaning, for her.

It was too late for her to go back to Hambro, but she could keep with her what she had taken from there when she married in 1917; my grandfather died in 1938, sure that his daughters were established and that the heaven of the Swedish Lutheran Church was imminent.

"If we ever go to Hambro," I said to her, "do you think Mr. Frank Lindquist would let me go for free to his movie house?"

"I don't see why not," she said.

At least, I tell myself now, I gave her excuses to bring out the piles of photographs. I can draw pictures of two neighborhoods now, my own in Milwaukee, and my mother's in Hambro. I can people them both accurately, even though the costumes are forty years apart in time. I know what boys wore when I was ten, and what they wore when my mother was ten.

She had a picture of her sister Claire taken shortly after she came to Chicago to begin, as it were, her life. She was only seventeen. She is posed against a dark background, her shoulders bare, but a frilly boa is gathered across her bosom for the sake of a careless, sultry kind of modesty. The ends of her hair are frizzed, distinctly seen, as are the frills of the boa. Her face is not made up. When I remember this picture I cannot avoid the association with publicity stills of silent-picture stars. It was shot for glamour, and achieved a cross between the vamp and a faintly voluptuous helplessness and innocence.

"She was pretty," I said to my mother.

"She did some modeling. She put every dollar she earned on her back for clothes," she said. I couldn't miss the disapproval. But she said then, as an afterthought to fairness perhaps, "Claire was the loveliest girl in Hambro."

I can understand my Aunt Claire. To a girl whose sisters were married and gone, her father strongly grained with Old World rigidity, the town of Hambro must have seemed created to escape from. It was a prison full-blown as soon as she knew that her beauty awed the Swedish farm boys.

At the time of our trip there, in 1949, when she was just over forty, and still very attractive, it may have been the only part of her life with much substance to it, since the bubble of her beauty had been popped, as it always is, by time.

Her marriage lasted only a year, somewhere in the middle twenties. She had no children, and no one spoke of her husband. Somewhere through the years I have absorbed the idea that he had some connection with speakeasies and bootlegging.

She kept company for a while with a man who was one of the victims of the St. Valentine's Day Massacre though she vowed the only inkling she had was the sedan he drove, which, though old, was capable of tremendous acceleration. She once told me he was a wonderful dancing partner.

Because she worked as a legal secretary, I never spent more than a weekend with her at her apartment. She had a small bar and liquor cabinet, and I was given sips when she mixed herself an old fashioned before dinner. She also had wine with her meals, constantly mentioned her efforts to watch her weight, and, unlike her sisters, did some entertaining.

She had a colored maid come in to set things up and serve. Elise, the maid, dressed in a black and white uniform, checked off each item as my aunt thought of it. Aunt Claire was the first of my relatives to have television, a huge console, and I sat and watched wrestling to keep out of the way.

"How's your soda?" she asked just before the guests arrived. She *always* had things like coke and Seven-Up in her small refrigerator, along with sparkling soda and sour mix in cases behind the kitchen door for mixing drinks.

"It's fine," I said. I was in my best clothes, and she had personally adjusted the tricornered fold in my breast-pocket handkerchief. She said that was the way a sharp dresser folded a hankie. She knew.

"Well, when they come, sweetie," she said to me—I never objected to *sweetie* from her—"you just act natural and eat anything you want. If you want more soda, you just ask Elise." I nodded, and she kissed me.

She held her cigarette, its cork tip smudged red with her lipstick, away from me to be sure I didn't get burned. With two aunts and so much traveling between them I was accustomed to receiving kisses from older women. Kisses were distinctive in themselves.

My Aunt Osa's kisses were very warm and pressing. She bent over and embraced me, hiding me in her arms, and suddenly there was a huge warm kiss on my mouth. My mother's kisses were a little nervous, a little sharp. She usually kissed twice to be sure it lasted. Aunt Claire's were the rarest, perhaps because she worried about her makeup.

She had just taken a puff of her cigarette, so she had to turn her head quickly to one side and blow out the smoke. With the heel of her other hand—her nail polish was not dry—she touched one of my cheeks, and on the other, bending over me in my chair, she put her lips.

Elise happened to pass through the living room just then. "I know the boy gets the most lovin' around here," she said.

"Isn't he a doll?" my aunt said.

The party is unimportant except to say that after I had met everyone—there were perhaps a dozen faces or more which inclined in my direction, a dozen hands with nail polish and rings on the fingers, the men's hands smooth, with big-faced watches on their wrists, a couple of polite questions as to how I liked staying with my auntie in Chicago, wasn't it keen?—I became bored because I had nothing to do once my stomach was bloated with coke and tiny sandwiches, olives, and nuts.

When no one was watching I slipped a cigarette from one of the boxes set out for the party and scurried into the bathroom and locked the door. I sat on the toilet and smoked, watching myself in the big mirror on the wall which was draped with an artistic fish net. It seems somehow right to me that I should have tasted my first vice at the hands of my Aunt Claire.

I remember. I remember the year before the trip, filled with allusions to Hambro, its people, the talk at the dinner table after dinner that Christmas when my aunts came to our house in Milwaukee. We all sat quietly at the table after eating, drinking egg coffee. I think all of us felt depressed when the last anecdote was over. "What we'll surely have to do is take a drive down to Hambro, Adolph," Aunt Osa said. "Do you know Grandma Sorenson will be ninety-four this coming year? Heavens, if Dad were alive, he'd be nearly a hundred today." It seemed to break their mood.

I suppose I was too busy eating cake, but I didn't react to what my mother said; she was saying how strange Hambro would seem now that Mrs. Swenson had passed away.

Spring came. Grandma Sorenson had her ninety-fourth birthday, and I had my twelfth. And we made our trip to Hambro, my aunts, my mother, myself, my Uncle Adolph driving.

There is not much to say of the town. It had been captured once as white houses and broad green lawns with swings and arbors, and then it had raced on with time. Now it was wide, paved streets, a supermarket, two traffic lights, and in the older section where Grandma Sorenson still lived in my grandfather's house—in the old manner, he willed it to her for her services to the family—it had become, frankly, a bit shabby.

Nothing was right. Bengt Berntson had split up his gun collection among his four sons, and the cabinet where he kept them was filled with dishes belonging to his wife. Thurston did not leave the house, even in good weather. His leg had been operated on again, shortened, and he sat day after day by the radio, probably going a little mad. He didn't talk much to my mother or my aunts, only once to me; we shook hands, and I was concerned whether or not my deportment was pleasing Uncle Adolph. He never mentioned the army. Mr. Frank Lindquist had sold the movie house and was an old man who sat in a chair and slapped his knee nervously while he spoke of dead people.

Everyone, everyone was old. Women my aunts said had been lovely girls with blond hair were gray and had moustaches I could see when the light was right. Men who had been handsome or soldiers or football players or the dirtiest boy in class, were retired, with large paunches and liver-spotted hands.

It must have been since before Aunt Claire left for Chicago, in the early twenties, that Grandma Sorenson had seen all three sisters together at one time. And then, she was ninety-four; it's not unkind to presume she was senile.

We went right in the front door of my grandfather's house, down a short hall, and my aunts and my mother went in to her in what was a small sun porch.

She was in a rocking chair, her hands folded over her lap. She was very fat, wore glasses, wrapped in an afghan to protect her from drafts. She looked up, saw my mother and my aunts, and spoke as though they had just come in from a walk downtown or a ride in someone's new motor car, as if it were thirty-five or forty years earlier.

"Oh," she said in her soft, whispering voice, "it's the Engstrom girls."

Here is the moment I want! My aunts and my mother cried, and under their influence I cried too. Perhaps I was tired from the drive, certainly flagged with disappointment at what I had found—not found—in the town. But I knew *why*, I *felt* why they cried, and of that I am proud. They cried after their own fashions: Aunt Osa generously, copiously, while smiling; my mother bitterly, with regret; Aunt Claire delicately, sparingly. It is a moment I know so well I will never forget it, and so I have stopped it, stopped time.

We visited the cemetery last of all. My mother stood with her feet apart and pointed out the graves to me. "Here's my mother," she said, "and here's your Grandfather Engstrom, Oskar."

But there was only the tombstone and the mound; I have no memory of my grandfather. And of the others, my mother, my aunts, Uncle Adolph, only I remain. But this much that I've told, this much is mine now. No matter what, all this is saved. This much is saved forever.

Hog's Heart

Nor mouth had, no nor mind, expressed
What heart heard of, ghost guessed

It is everything and it is nothing. Hog says, "Different times, it's different feeling. Sometimes I feel like that it might could just be a feeling. Sometimes, I feel it is happening right then."

"Goddamnit, Hog," says Dr. Odie Anderson. Hog, perched on the edge of the examination table, cannot be more precise. He feels ridiculous, feet suspended above the floor like a child's, wearing a flimsy paper hospital gown that, like a dress, barely covers his scarred knees. Though the air-conditioning sighs incessantly, he exudes a light sweat, pasting the gown to his skin, thighs and buttocks cemented to the table's chill metal surface. "Is it pains?" the doctor says. "Is it chest pain? Is it pain in your arm or shoulder? Is it pain you feel in your neck or your jaw?"

Hog says, "It might could be I just imagine it sometimes." Dr. Odie Anderson, team physician, sits in his swivel chair, lab coat thrown open, collar unbuttoned, necktie askew, feet up and crossed on his littered desk. Hog sees the holes in the soles of the doctor's shoes. Odie Anderson's head lolls slightly, canted. His eyes, bulging and glossy, like a man with arrested goiter, roll. He licks his lips, moistens the rim of scraggly beard around his open mouth.

"Damn," says Dr. Anderson, "is it choking? Your breath hard to get? Sick to your stomach a lot?" To avoid looking at him, Hog turns his head to the window before opening his eyes. The rectangle of searing morning light dizzies him. He grips the edge of the table with both hands, tries not to hear the doctor, feels the trickle of sweat droplets course downward from the tonsure of hair above his jug ears, from the folds of flesh at his throat, the sausage rolls of fat at the back of his neck, from his armpits. He represses malarial shudders as the air conditioner blows on his bare back where the paper gown gaps.

"You want me to send you to Jackson to the hospital? Want all kinds of tests, swallowing radioactivity so they can take movies of your veins?" Almost touching the windowpane, magnolia leaves shine in the brilliant light as if greased. One visible blossom looks molded of dull white wax that will surely melt and run if the sun's rays reach it. A swath of lawn shimmers in the heat like green fire. The length of sidewalk Hog can see is empty. The cobbled street beyond is empty, stones buckled and broken.

"Not now," Hog says. "I got a season starting. I might could maybe go come spring if I can get off recruiting awhile."

"Well now," Dr. Anderson is saying, "you *are* fat as a damn house, Hog, and your blood pressure *is* high. You might could be a classic case, except you don't smoke, and last I heard your daddy's still kicking up there to Hot Coffee."

"Daddy's fine. He's a little bitty man, though. I come by my size favoring Mama's people." A pulpcutter's truck, stacked high with pine logs, and a flatbed truck, stumps chained to the bed, pass on their way up to the Masonite plant at Laurel.

"Get dressed, Hog," the doctor says. "I can't find nothing wrong in there. Hell, you strong as stump whiskey and mean as a yard dog!" Hog buttons his shirt, zips his fly evading Dr. Anderson's leering cackle.

Sometimes it is everything. It is the sticky, brittle feel of sweat drying on his skin, the drafty breath of the air conditioner that makes him shudder in spasms, raises goose bumps on his forearms. It is the late August morning's heat and humidity hovering like a cloud outside, waiting to drop on him, clutch him. It is the baked streets and sidewalks, the withering campus and lawns, everyone in Hattiesburg driven indoors until dusk brings relief from the glaring sun of south Mississippi.

"Say hey to Nyline and the chaps for me," says Odie Anderson.

It is his wife and four sons, it is the steaming campus, the athletic dormitory and stadium, the office where his senior assistants wait to review game films, the approach of the season opener at home against Alabama, this fourth year of his five-year contract, two-a-day workouts and recruiting trips across the Deep South and a pending NCAA investigation. It is all things now and up to now—his folks up at Hot Coffee, paying his dues coaching high school and junior college, his professional career cut short by injury in Canada, all things seeming to have come together to shape his conviction that he will soon die from heart failure.

"We going to whip up on Bama, Hog?"

"We die trying," says Hog. They laugh. It is nothing.

Hog decides he is not dying, not about to, not subject to be dying. It is something that is probably nothing, and because he cannot define or express it, it is a terror there is no point in fearing. Hog decides it is himself, Hog Hammond, alive in Hattiesburg, Mississippi, in the blistering heat of late August, knowing he is alive, no more than naturally wondering about death.

Fraternity and sorority pep-club banners limply drape the stadium walls. BEAT BAMA. ROLL BACK THE TIDE. GO SOUTHERN. WE BACK HOG'S BOYS. The stadium walls throw heat into Hog's face. Pines and magnolias and live oaks droop in the humidity. The mockingbirds are silent. The painted letters on the banners swim before his eyes, air pressing him like a leaden mist. He begins to consciously reach, pull for each breath, lurches sweating, wheezing, into the shade of the stadium entrance to his office.

Inside, the dimness makes him light-blind, the coolness is a clammy shock, his heaving echoes off tile and paneling. Hog finds himself, eyes adjusting, before the Gallery of Greats, a wall-length display of photos and newspaper clippings, trophies and pennants, locked behind nonreflecting glass. This pantheon of Mississippi Southern's finest athletes, record-setters, semi-All Americans, is a vanity he cannot resist.

His breathing slows and softens, sweat drying in his clothes, on his skin, as he steps closer. There he is, the great Hog Hammond in the prime of his prowess and renown. Three pictures of Hog: a senior, nineteen years ago, posed in half-crouch, helmet off to show his bullet head, cropped hair, arms raised shoulder-high, fingers curled like talons, vicious animal snarl on his glistening face; Hog, nineteen years ago, down in his three-point stance, right arm lifting to whip the shiver-pad into the throat of an imaginary offensive guard; Hog, snapped in action, the legendary Alabama game nineteen years ago, charging full-tilt, only steps away from brutally dumping the confused Alabama quarterback for a loss. Hog is motion, purpose, power; the Alabama quarterback is static, timid, doomed.

The newspaper clippings are curled at the edges, yellowing. *Southern Shocks Ole Miss. Southern Stalemates Mighty Tide. The Hog Signs For Canada Pros.*

Athletic Director Tub Moorman is upon him, comes up behind him silently, like an assassin with a garrote, the only warning the quick stink of the dead cigar he chews, laced with the candy odor of his talc and hair oil. Hog feels a catch in his throat, a twinge in his sternum, salivates.

"Best not live on old-timey laurels, Hog," says Athletic Director Tub Moorman. A column of nausea rises from the pit of Hog's belly to his chest, tip swaying into his gullet like a cottonmouth's head. He tenses to hold his windpipe open. "Best look to *this* season," Tub Moorman says. Hog, pinned against the cool glass of the Gallery of Greats, gags, covers with a cough.

"I'm directly this minute subject to review game films," he is able to say. Tub Moorman does not seem to hear. He is a butterball, head round as a washpot, dirt-gray hair slicked with reeking tonic, florid face gleaming with aftershave. He dresses like a New Orleans pimp, white shoes, chartreuse slacks, loud blazer, gaudy jewel in his wide tie, gold digital watch, oversize diamond on his fat pinky, glossy manicured nails. His sour breath cuts through his lotions. He limps slightly from chronic gout.

"This year four," Tub Moorman says. "Year one we don't much care do you win. Play what you find when you come aboard.

Year two, year three, your business to scout the ridges and hollows for talent. Year four, we looking to see do you *produce*, see do we want to keep you in the family after year five. This is year four. Root hog or die, hear?" The athletic director speaks, laughs, without removing his unlit cigar from his mouth. Hog can see the slimey butt of the cigar, Tub Moorman's tongue and stained teeth.

Hog is able to say, "I'm feeling a touch puny today," before he must clamp his lips.

"You know we mighty high on you, Hog," Tub Moorman says. "You one of us and all." He flicks his lizard's eyes at the Gallery's pictures and clippings. "You a great one. You hadn't got injured so soon in Canada, you might could of been famous as a professional. We fixing to build this program up great, Hog. Fixing to find the man can do it if you ain't him."

"I'm subject to give it all I got," Hog gasps, bile in his mouth.

"Fact is," says the athletic director, "you got to beat Alabama or Ole Miss or Georgia Tech or Florida, somebody famous, or we got to be finding us the man will."

"I might could. I got me a nigger place-kicker can be the difference."

Tub Moorman's laugh is a gurgling, like the flush of a sewer. "We ain't particular," he says, "but the NCAA is. Best not let no investigators find out your Cuba nigger got a forged transcript, son. Best forget old-timey days, be up and doing *now*." Hog hurries to the nearest toilet, the athletic director's stench clings to him, chest-thick with sickness, throat charged with acid, head swimming. Retching into the closest commode, Hog blows and bellows like a teased bull, clears the residue of Tub Moorman's smell from his nostrils.

On the portable screen Alabama routs Ole Miss before a record homecoming crowd at Oxford. Slivers of the sunlight penetrate the room at the edges of the blackout curtains, casting an eery light on the acoustical ceiling. The projector chatters, the air conditioner chugs. Only Sonny McCartney, Hog's coordinator, takes notes, writing a crabbed hand into manila folders, calling for freeze-frames and reruns. Sonny McCartney reminds Hog frequently that national ranking is only a matter of planning, implementation of strategy, time.

Wally Everett, offensive assistant, mans the projector. Once a fleet wide receiver for the Tarheels of North Carolina, he wears a prim, superior expression on his patrician face. Because he wears a jacket and necktie in even the warmest weather, he is sometimes mistaken for a professor. Believing there is no excuse for vulgar or obscene language, on or off the playing field, he is a frequent speaker at Fellowship of Christian Athletes banquets. He sits up straight in his chair, knees crossed, like a woman, hands, when not operating the projector's levers and buttons, folded in his lap.

The defensive assistant, Thumper Lee, slouches in a chair at the back of the room. He played a rugged nose-guard for a small Baptist college in Oklahoma, looks like an aging ex-athlete should, unkempt, strong, moody, unintellectual. He shifts his weight in his chair, stamps his feet often as Alabama's three-deep-at-every-position squad shreds the Rebels on the screen. He snorts, says, "I seen two county fairs and a train, but I ain't never seen nothing like them! Them sumbitches *good*, Hog!"

"The problem," says Sonny McCartney, "is to decide what we can do best against them."

"They execute to perfection," says Wally Everett.

Wally rewinds the film for one more showing. Sonny rereads his notes. Thumper Lee spits a stream of juice from his Red Man cud into the wastebasket. The room is darker with the projector bulb off, the air conditioner louder in the greater silence. Hog holds tightly to the arms of his chair. He feels as if, at the very center of his heart, a hole, a spot of nothingness, forms. He braces himself. The hole at the center of his heart doubles in size, doubles again; his vital, central substance is disappearing, vanishing without a trace. He tries to hear the movement of his blood, but there is only the perpetual churning of the air conditioner, the click and snap of the projector being readied.

"Hog," says Thumper Lee, pausing to rise an inch off his chair, break wind with a hard vibrato, "Hog, they going to eat our lunch come opening day."

"Every offense has a defense," Sonny McCartney says.

"There is little argument with basic execution," Wally says.

It will grow, Hog believes, this void in his chest, until he remains, sitting, a hollow shell with useless arms, legs, head. He will crumple, fall to the carpeted floor, dead.

"Alabama don't know we got Fulgencio Carabajal," Sonny says.

"Neither does the NC double-A," Wally says. "Yet. But they will if we let just one person close enough to speak to him."

"Is that tutoring learning him any English yet?" Thumper Lee asks.

"Again?" says Wally, finger on the projector's start-button.

"Ain't this a shame?" says Thumper, "Our best offense a nigger from Cuba don't talk no English."

"*I* did not forge his transcript," Wally says.

"He *can* kick," says Sonny, and, "Hog?"

Hog, dying, rises from his chair. "You-all discuss this without me," he says, finds he can take a step toward the door. Another. "I got to get me some fresh air, I am feeling puny, boys," says Hog, reaches the door, opens it, leaves, walking slowly, carefully, like a man made of blown glass, no core left to him at all, no heart.

There is no reason Hog should wake in the still-dark hours of early morning, no stomach upset or troubling dream. At first he is merely awake, Nyline beside him. Then his eyes focus, show him the lighter darkness, false dawn at the bedroom windows, and then he sees the ceiling, walls, furniture, the glow of the nightlight from the master bedroom's full bath, the light blanket covering him and his wife, Nyline in silhouette, the back of her head studded with curlers. He hears the gentle growl of her snoring. He hears the high sighing of cooled air cycling through the house on which the mortgage runs past the year 2000.

He lies very still in the king-size bed, shuts out what he can see and hear, the rich smell of Nyline's Shalimar perfume, closes himself away, then knows what has awakened him from deep sleep. Now Hog hears, measures the rhythms, recognizes the subtle reduction in pace, tempo, intensity of his heartbeat. His heart is slowing, and this has awakened him, so that he can die knowing he is dying. The beat is still regular, but there comes a minuscule hesitation, a near-catch, a stutter before the muffled thump of each beat. He lies very still, holds his breath, the better to hear and feel. Then he inches his left hand free of the cover, moves it into position to press the declining pulse in his right wrist.

His heart will run down like a flywheel yielding up its motion to the darkness of the master bedroom. He is dying here and now, at the moment of false dawn that shows him the shafts of pine trunks in his yard, the wrinkled texture of his new lawn of bermuda grass. He will lie there and be discovered by Nyline when she wakes to the electric buzz of the alarm on her bedside table.

"Nyline," Hog whispers. "Nyline." His voice surprises him; how long can a man speak, live, on the momentum of his last heartbeats? "Nyline." She groans, turns to him, puts out a hand, eyes shut, groping. Her arm comes across his chest, takes hold of his shoulder. She nuzzles his jaw, kisses him in her half-sleep, presses her head into his throat, her curlers stabbing the soft flesh.

Hog says, "Nyline, I love you. I thank you for marrying me, when my people is just redneck pulpcutters and you're from fine high-type Biloxi people. It is always a wonder to me why you married me when I was just a football player, and you was runnerup Miss Gulf Coast and all. There's mortgage life insurance on the house, Nyline, so you'll have the house all paid for."

"Big sweet thing," his wife mumbles into his collarbone.

"No, Nyline," he says. "I do love you and thank you for giving me our boys. I am dying, Nyline, and it is just as good I do now, because we won't be beating Alabama or Ole Miss nor nobody big-timey, and the NCAA will likely soon get me for giving a scholarship to a Cuba nigger has to have a interpreter to play football, and we will lose this house and everything, except I am dying and you will get it because of insurance."

"Lovey, you want me to be sweet for you?" Nyline says, kisses his hairy chest, strokes his face and the slick bald crown of his head.

"No," Hog says. "Listen, Nyline. Tell me can you hear my heart going." She mutters as he turns her head gently, places her ear against his breast, then resumes her light snoring.

Dying, Hog lifts her away to her side of the bed, throws back the cover, rises, pads out of the master bedroom. Dying, he walks down the hall to the bedrooms where his four sons sleep.

He can stand at the end of the hall, look into both bedrooms, see them sleeping, two in each room, and he stands, looking upon the future of his name and line, stands thinking of his wife and sons, how he loves them, in his wonderful new home with a mortgage that runs beyond the year 2000, thinking it is cruel to die when he can see the future sleeping in the two bedrooms.

It is the coming of true dawn, flaring in the windows of his sons' side-by-side bedrooms, that grants him a reprieve. True dawn comes, lights the trees and grass and shrubbery on his lawn, stirs a mockingbird to its first notes high in a pine tree, primes his flickering heart to a renewed rhythm. He feels it kick into vigor like a refueled engine, then goes to the hall bathroom, sits, grateful, weeping, on the edge of the bathtub, staring at his blank-white toes and toenails, lavender-tinged white feet, his heart resuming speed and strength for another day.

Nyline and his sons are somewhere outside with Daddy and Brother-boy, seeing the new machinery shed or feeding Brother-boy's catfish. Hog's mama serves him a big square of cornbread and a glass of cold buttermilk.

The golden cornbread, straight from the oven, radiates heat like a small sun. Hog bites, chews, swallows, breaks into a sweat as he chills his mouth with buttermilk. Not hungry, he gives himself over to the duty of eating for her. He sweats more freely with the effort, feels a liquid warmth emerge in his belly, grow. Hog feigns gusto, moans, smacks his lips, slurps for her. A viscous heat squirts into his chest.

"No more," he says as she reaches toward the pan with a knife to cut him another helping. "Oh, please, Mama, no," says Hog. He tries to smile.

"I want to know what is the matter with my biggest boy," she says. "You say you are feeling some puny, but I know my boy, Euliss. I think you are troubled in your spirit, son."

"I have worries, Mama," he tells her. "We got to play Alabama. I am just troubled with my work."

"Is it you and Nyline? Is it your family, Euliss, something with my grandbabies?"

"We all fine, Mama. Truly." He averts his eyes. She does not look right, his old mama, in this modern kitchen, chrome and formica and plastic-covered chairs, double oven set in the polished brick wall, blender built into the counter top, bronze-tone refrigerator big as two football lockers, automatic icecube maker, frostless, Masonite veneer on the cupboards; Hog remembers her cooking at an iron woodstove, chopping wood for it as skillfully as she took the head off a chicken while he clung to her long skirts, sucking a sugartit. He remembers her buying fifty-pound blocks of ice from the nigger wagon driver from Laurel, taking his tongs and carrying it into the house herself (because she would not allow a nigger in her kitchen) until Hog was old enough to fetch and carry for her, his daddy out in the woods cutting pulp timber dawn to dusk.

Hog covers his eyes with his hand to hide the start of tears, hurt and joy mixing in him like a boiling pot, that his mama has this fine kitchen in this fine new brick home built by his daddy and Brother-boy on a loan secured by Hog's signature and Hog's life insurance, that his mama is old and will not ever again be like he remembers her, that she will not live forever.

"I do believe my boy is troubled in his soul," Mama says.

"Not my soul, Mama." Hog comes by his size from Mama's daddy, a pulpcutter who died before Hog was born; Hog remembers her telling him how her daddy had lost four and a half fingers from his two hands, cutting pulpwood for Masonite in Laurel all his life until a tree fell on him and killed him. Hog looks at her fingers, at his own.

"Are you right with Jesus, Euliss?" she says. She leans across the table, hands clenched in prayer now. "I pray to Jesus," says mama, "for my boy Euliss. I pray for him each day and at meeting particular." A dam bursts somewhere on the margins of Hog's interior, a deluge of tepidness rushing to drown his heart.

"We go to church regular in Hattiesburg, Mama," he is able to say before the spill deprives him of words and will.

"Pray with me, Euliss," she says. "Oh, pray Jesus ease your trouble, drive doubt and Satan out! Oh, I am praying to You, Jesus, praying up my biggest boy to You!" Her locked hands shake, as if she tries to lift a weight too great for her wiry arms, her eyes squeezed shut to see only Blessed Jesus, lips puckered as though she drew the Holy Spirit into her lungs. Hog cannot look. It is his old mama, who attends the Primitive Baptist Church of Hot Coffee, where she wrestles Satan until she falls, frothing, weeping, to the floor before the tiny congregation, where she washes the feet of elders. "Jesus, Jesus, speak to my boy Euliss," she prays in the fine modern kitchen of the modern brick ranch house built on land won by two generations of scrub cattle drivers and pulpwood cutters.

Hog's heart moves like a wellhouse pump lifting a thick, hot sweetness into his mouth. This death is sweet, filling, filled with Mama's love, all he feels of his memories of her, Daddy, Brother-boy. "JesuspleaseJesusplease," she chants.

"Mama," says Hog, getting up, voice breaking on his lips like a bubble of honey, "I got to go find Daddy and Nyline and Brother-boy and those chaps. We got to be leaving back to Hattiesburg. Time flying, Mama." He leaves the kitchen, the waters of her love receding in his wake.

Hog and his daddy admire the glossy Angus at the saltlick, the cattle clustering in the narrow shade of the old mule-driven mill where Hog helped his daddy crush cane for syrup. Hog sees the Angus melded with the scrubby mavericks he ran in the woods with razorbacks for his daddy, hears the squeak and crunch of the mill turning, snap of cane stalks. "Now see this, Euliss," says his daddy, a small man who has aged by shriveling, drying, hardening. "Don't it beat all for raising a shoat in a nigger-rigged crib?" his hardness glowing redly in the terrible sunshine, burnished with pride over the new cement floor of his pigpen. Hog, gasping, clucks appreciation for him. "Wait and see Brother-boy feed them fish!" his daddy says.

"Daddy," Hog says, "how come Mama's so much for churching and you never setting foot in it, even for revivals?" Hog's daddy blows his nose between thumb and forefinger, expertly flicks snot into the grass near the row of humming beehives that Hog, wreathed in smoke, veiled, helped rob in his youth.

"I never held to it," his daddy says, stopped by Hog's heavy hand on his shoulder.

"Why not? You didn't never believe in God? Ain't you never been so scared of dying or even of living so's you wanted to pray like Mama?" He hears his own voice muffled, as if cushioned by water.

"I never faulted her for it, Euliss," says his daddy. And, "And no man dast fault me for not. Son, most of us don't get hardly no show in life. Now, not you, but me and Brother-boy and your mama. Life wearies a man. Them as needs Jesusing to die quiet in bed or wherever, I say fine, like for Mama. Me nor mine never got no show, excepting you, naturally, Euliss, a famous player and coach and all. I guess I can die withouten I screech to Jesus."

"Daddy," says Hog. Blood fills his chest, a rich lake about his heart, pressing his lungs. "Daddy, was I a good boy?"

"Now, Euliss." His daddy embraces him, sinewy arms, the spread fingers of his rough hands clasping Hog's heaving sides. "Euliss, don't you know I have bragged on you since you was a chap?"

"Are you proud of me still?" His daddy laughs, releases him, steps back.

"Oh, you was a pistol, son, for that football from the start. I recollect you not ten years old going out to lift the new calf day by day to build muscles for football playing!"

"Daddy." He feels a pleasant cleft in his breast widen, a tide of blood.

"Recollect the time I *told* you not to be blocking yourself into the gallery post for football practice? I had to frail you with a stick. Oh, son, you was a pure pistol for that footballin! Your daddy been bragging on you since, Euliss!"

"Find Brother-boy. Want to see them fish," Hog chokes, this death almost desirable to him. He moves away, suffocating in the fluid of his emotions.

"Brother," says Hog, "Brother-boy, are you resentful you stayed and lived your life here? Ain't you never wanted a wife and chaps of your own? Do you resent I went away to school for football and to Canada for my own life while you just stayed working for Daddy?" Brother-boy looks like Hog remembers himself half a dozen years ago, less bald, less overweight. From a large cardboard drum, he scoops meal, sows it on the dark green surface of the artificial pond. The catfish he farms swim to the top, thrash, feeding, rile the pond into bubbles and spray. "Was I a good brother to you? Is it enough I signed a note so's you can start a fish farm and all this cattle and stock of Daddy's?"

Brother-boy, sowing the meal in wide arcs over the pond, says, "I never grudged you all the fine things you got, Euliss. You been a special person, famous playing football in college and Canada and now a famous coach." His brother's voice dims, lost in the liquid whip of the pond's surface, the frenzied feeding of the catfish. "I am a happy enough man, Euliss," says Brother-boy. "I have things I do. Mama and Daddy need me. They getting old, Euliss. I don't need me no wife nor chaps, and I got a famous big brother was a famous player once and now a coach, and your sons are my nephews." Hog remembers Brother-boy, a baby wearing a shift, a chap following after him at chores, coming to see him play for Jones Agricultural Institute & Junior College in Laurel, for Mississippi Southern, once coming by train and bus all the way up to Calgary to see Hog's career end in injury. "It is not my nature to resent nor grudge nobody nothing," says his brother. "It is my way to accept what is."

Hog lurches away, seeking an anchor for his heart, tossed in a wave of sweet blood, wishing he could die here and now if he must die. But knowing his death is yet to come is like a dry wind that evaporates the splash of love and memory within him, turning this nectar stale, then sour.

Seeking an overview of the last full drill in pads, Hog takes to a stubby knoll, shaded by a live oak tree, its long snaking limbs supported by cables fastened to the tree's black trunk. From here, the practice field falls into neat divisions of labor.

At the far end of the field, parallel to the highway to Laurel and Hot Coffee, chimeric behind the rising heat waves, Fulgencio Carabajal placekicks ball after ball through jerry-built wooden goalposts, the first-string center snapping, third-team quarterback holding, two redshirts to shag balls for the Cuban, who takes a break every dozen or so balls to talk with his interpreter. Hog watches Fulgencio's soccer-style approach, hears the hollow strike of the side of his shoe on the ball, the pock of this sound a counterpoint to the beating of Hog's heart. He tries to follow the ball up between the uprights, loses it in the face of the sun that washes out the green of the dry grass.

Closest to Hog's shady knoll, the first- and second-team quarterbacks alternate short spot-passes with long, lazy bombs to a self-renewing line of receivers who wait their turns casually, hands on hips. Catching balls in long fly patterns, receivers trot up to the base of Hog's knoll, cradling the ball loosely, showboating for him. He does not allow them to think he notices. The slap of ball in hands comes as if deliberately timed to the throb of his heart, adding its emphasis to the twist of its constrictions.

At the field's center, Sonny McCartney coordinates, wears a gambler's green eyeshade, clipboard and ballpoint in hand. Sonny moves from offense to defense in the shimmer of the heat like a man wading against a current. Hog squints to find Thumper Lee, on his knees to demonstrate firing off the snap to his noseguard, his jersey as sweated as any player's. Wally Everett, as immobile as Hog, stands among his offensive players, stopping the drill frequently with his whistle, calling them close for short lectures, as unperturbed by the temperature and humidity as if he worked with chalk on blackboard in an air-conditioned classroom.

Hog's heart picks up its pace, the intensity of each convulsion increasing to a thud, a bang. Now he cannot distinguish the echo of his accelerating heartbeat from the smack of pads down on the practice field, the slap of ball on sweaty palm, thumping of the tackling dummy, crash of shoulders against the blocking sled, squealing springs, the hollow pock of Fulgencio Carabajal's kicking.

Hog closes his eyes to die, digs with his cleats for a firmer stance on the knoll, prepared to topple into the dusty grass. He tenses, wonders why this raucous slamming of his heart does not shake him, why he does not explode into shards of flesh and bone. And wonders why he is not dead, still holding against his chest's vibrations, when he hears Sonny McCartney blow the final whistle to end the drill. Hog's heart subsides with the blood's song in his ears, like the fade of Sonny's whistle in the super-heated air of late afternoon.

It is light. Light falling upon Hog, his wife still sleeping as he rises. Special, harder and brighter light while fixing himself a quick breakfast in the kitchen, chrome trim catching and displaying early morning's show of light to him while Nyline is dressing, his sons stirring in their bedrooms toward this new day. Light, the morning sky clear as creek water, climbing sun electric-white, overwhelming Hog's sense of trees, houses, streets, driving slowly through Hattiesburg to the stadium. And light, lighting his consciousness, pinning his attention in the gloom of the squad's locker room, the last staff strategy session, his talk to his players before they emerge into the light of the stadium.

Hog tells them, "It is not just football or playing a game. It is like life. It is mental toughness. Or you might call it confidence. I do not know if you-all are as good as Alabama. Newspapers and TV say you are not, they will whip our butts. If it is true, they is nothing any of us or you-all can do. We all have to face that. It is Alabama we are playing today. Maybe it is like you-all have to go out and play them knowing you will not have any show. It might could be I am saying mental toughness is just having it in you to do it even knowing they will whip up on your butt. I don't know no more to say." He leads them out into the light.

He sees, hears, registers it all, but all is suffused with this light, a dependency of light. The game flows like impure motes in perfect light. The game is exact, concrete, but still dominated by, a function of this light. The opening game against Alabama is a play of small shadows within the mounting intensity of light.

At the edge of the chalked boundary, Hog notes the legendary figure of the opposing coach across the field, tall, chainsmoking cigarettes, houndstooth-checked hat, coatless in the dense heat Hog does not feel. This light has no temperature for Hog, a light beyond heat or cold.

"They eating our damn lunch, Hog!" Thumper Lee screams in his ear when Alabama, starting on their twenty after Fulgencio Carabajal sends the kickoff into the endzone bleachers, drives in classic ground-game fashion for the first touchdown. The snap is mishandled, the kick wide.

"I declare we can run wide on them, Hog," says Wally Everett as Southern moves the ball in uneven spurts to the Crimson Tide thirty-seven, where, stalled by a broken play, Fulgencio Carabajal effortlessly kicks the three-pointer. "I have seen teams field-goaled to death," Wally says.

Late in the second quarter, Southern trails only 13–9 after Fulgencio splits the uprights from fifty-six yards out. "We *got* the momentum, Hog," says Sonny McCartney, earphones clamped on to maintain contact with the press-box spotters. "We can run wide, and pray Fulgencio don't break a leg."

Thumper Lee, dancing, hugging the necks of his tackles, spits, screams, "I seen a train and two fairs, but I ain't never seen *this* day before!"

"Notice the Bear's acting nervous over there?" Wally says, points to the excited assistants clustering in quick conference on the houndstooth hat across the field.

Says Hog, "You can't never tell nothing about how it's going to be."

His death comes as light, all light, clarity, comprehensive and pervasive. There is nothing Hog does not see, hear, know. Everything is here, in this light, and not here. It is a moment obliterating moments, time or place.

He knows a great legend is unfolding on the playing field, an upset of the Crimson Tide. Hog knows he has come to this wonder, this time and place, by clear chronology, sequence of accident and design, peopled since the beginning with his many selves and those who have marked him and made him who and what he is in this instant of his death. Light draws him in, draws everything together in him, Hog, the context of his death.

Dr. Odie Anderson sits on a campstool behind the players' bench, feet up on the bench, scratching his beard with both hands, rolling his bulged eyes at the scoreboard. Athletic Director Tub Moorman's face is wine-red with excitement, his unlit cigar chewed to pulp. Thumper Lee drools tobacco juice when he shouts out encouragement to his stiffening defense. Wally Everett smirks as he counsels his quarterback. Sonny McCartney relays information from his spotters in the press-box, where Nyline and the four sons of Hog watch the game through binoculars, drinking complimentary Coca-Colas. On the bench next to his chattering interpreter, Fulgencio Carabajal waits indifferently for his next field-goal attempt. In the new modern kitchen in Hot Coffee, Hog's people, Mama, Daddy, Brotherboy listen to the radio broadcast, proud and praying. Only a little farther, folded into his memory, are the many Hogs that make him Hog: a boy in Hot Coffee lifting new calves to build muscle, football find at the Jones Agricultural Institute & Junior College, bonafide gridiron legendary Little All-American on this field, sure-fire prospect with Calgary's Stampeders in the Canadian Football League, career cut short by knee and ankle injuries, high-school coach, defensive assistant, coordinator, Hog here and now, head coach at Mississippi Southern University, all these simultaneous in the marvel of his death's light.

Dying, Hog looks into the glare of the sun, finds his death is not pain or sweetness, finds totality and transcendence, dies as they rush to where he lies on the turf, dying, accepting this light that is the heart of him joining all light, Hog and not-Hog, past knowing and feeling or need and desire to say it is only light, dies hearing Fulgencio Carabajal say, "*Es muerte?*" gone into such light as makes light and darkness one.

Macklin's Epigraphic Loss

Did you hear the one about the man who was so thin he fell through a hole in the seat of his pants and strangled?

To make an omelette, you have to break eggs

"What health problems do you associate with your obesity?"

"I tire easily. I'm short of breath all the time. I get a lot of headaches." The slightest exertion overheats me. I dread spring and summer, early autumn. April's breezes coat me in fine sweat that evaporates only with the first polar front. Any heat wave's a flannel suit I have to wear; I fear I'll melt. My ears ring constantly, high blood pressure. My overworked circulation beats out migraines at my temples. My body fluids simmer in May, worry to a full boil through June, July, August, subside to troubled bubbling after Labor Day, cool mercifully in the icy blasts of November.

In my dreams my weight continues to escalate. See myself: in my king-size reinforced bed, inflating like a bladder. My balloon body rises from the bed, floats to the ceiling, bobs, trapped. Mama and Sister scream out in horror. I wake to my shrill alarm. Sometimes my density increases with my bulk, gradually collapsing the mattress, which folds over me like a chasm closing after an earthquake. I burst through the floor and foundation. My alarm, Mama and Sister shrieking, calls to me from out of an endless dark. I measure my death, ounce by ounce, accumulating on my aching bones.

"In what ways is your day-by-day behavior limited by your obesity? Be frank, please."

"Well. I can't do normal things." I can eat, drink, sleep, talk, read and write. An average city block or one flight of stairs exhausts me. My heart thunders under my ribs. My vision blurs, ears sing, lungs heave like bellows. I love my family.

I don't dare run. Ordinary chairs are impossible. I can't fit behind the wheel of an automobile. Other than sharing TV with Mama, listening to Sister's records, I have no hobby, no recreation. I have no social life. No sex life. I must be seated to urinate. I haven't seen my genitals in several years.

I like to eat, drink, sleep, read, think. I'm an excellent student, expect to complete my dissertation in quantitative analysis before the end of this calendar year. I love my family.

If I could, I'd be outgoing with strangers. I'm hidden behind this wall. The wall gets thicker each day. I'm an object of humor, of pity, of scorn and contempt, of thinly veiled disgust. I have normal desires. I think I'll die soon. I'm killing myself, digging my grave with my teeth. My *Angst* is so blatant as to be inadmissible to others. I'm in terror of receiving an attractive offer from a carnival sideshow. I want a life. I'd rather die than live like this.

"Mr. Macklin, can you fix a particular date as the onset of your condition?"

"No." Ten pounds at birth. Mama likes to recall her astonishment when the doctor told her. Yet says she was no bigger with me than with Sister. Papa was proud. My baby pictures show a head round as a pot, chubby arms and legs. Toddling, I was burly, no-necked. In grammar school, already the brunt of cruel jeering. *Fatty-fatty boom-boom. Fatty, fatty, two-by-four, can't get through the bathroom door, had to do it on the floor.* Distinctly vicious in adolescence. *Lard ass. Wide sides. Looky, Macklin's got tits! Hey, Macklin, loan me a wrinkle, my girl's busy tonight.* Last echoes in college. *Baby Huey. Humphrey Pennyworth. Mr. Five-by-five!*

"What efforts have you made to reduce your weight prior to this occasion, Mr. Macklin?"

"Nothing worked." Everything. Laxatives caused hemorrhoids. Bulking agents, cellulose tablets designed to swell up inside the stomach, but I could always find room. Calorie-counting until I read *Calories Don't Count,* but they did. Grapefruit puckered my lips, burned my tongue and throat, turned my urine acid. Low-carbohydrate-high-fat regimens, all the butter and oil I could stand. My gullet felt greased. Pissing on chemically treated slips of paper to see if I could keep my system in ketosis. Fat clubs where we gave prizes, levied small fines for cheaters. A spa with pool, massage, steam, belts that jarred my kidneys, revolving drums studded with knobs battered my buttocks. Fish and green vegetable menus hawked by amoral corporations. You name it.

To a point. I won't have adipose tissue surgically removed, will not ask a dentist to wire my jaws shut, refuse to have my large intestine by-passed. I have integrity.

"Do you fully appreciate the loss we're contemplating, Mr. Macklin?"

"I think so." 489 down to 170. Way over half myself. I have a positive attitude. It's a search. Down there, deep inside. Waiting to be discovered. Come forth and be recognized. Complete his dissertation. Build a career. Have friends, date girls, court and marry. Children, a home. Weekends and holidays we'll visit relatives; vacations we'll travel. Love and be loved.

My two most frequent fantasies of death are: my body stolen by medical students for dissection and analysis; my body buried in a piano case, lowered to rest by a winch and boom, covered by a bulldozer.

"Other instances of obesity in your family?"

"None." Sister's a sylph, too thin for her own good. Mama's large, but big-boned, well able to carry it. Papa was average. He died of simple coronary occlusion. I love my family.

"Professor Stocker will see you now, Mr. Macklin." I'm dying. I'm afraid to die. I want to kill myself. I want life. I hear myself saying these things.

A minute on your lips, forever on your hips

Mama's in the kitchen before I wake. I wake with enthusiasm, troubled only by a nagging itch at the back of my consciousness that I attribute to dreaming's residue. My ears perk to the tap and rattle of Mama busy at the stove, the maudlin music of Sister's records a comfortable background. My nostrils flare at the aroma of rich frying slithering under my door. Dressed, washing up, Sister's music is louder, the swelling sound of Mama's preparations crowding the bathroom with me. The run and flush of water cannot dilute them.

"Good morning, Mama." I kiss her. Her worn robe's pathetic, slippers flopping, greying hair pinned back. Her smile, her eyes love me to love her for another day.

"Is my big boy hungry?" I'm lost, inundated in the panorama of Mama's bounty arrayed on the bright tablecloth. The odors make congress in the sunny air, something deep and rich, softly viscous, into which I fall as I take my place. Oh my loving mother! The itch begins to subside. I scarcely notice Sister take her seat across the groaning board from me. Mama hovers, passing and dishing, cooing her rapture.

A platter of slippery eggs, over-easy, gold yolks running like arteries at the touch of my fork. Mama deftly slides five onto my gleaming plate. Cooked in one hundred percent pure, sweet, creamery butter. "You know I hate eggs," Sister says as I reach for toast. Mama's homemade whole wheat, sliced thick and ragged, toasted crunchy on the surface, nutty-mushy within. I apply chunks of refrigerator-hard butter, an artist creating textured surface with a palette knife. I use it for a plow to heap my fork, sop up pools of stiffening yolk. Half a dozen slices does it. Alternated with wedges of whole-hog sausage, country style, flecked with kernels of hot pepper that sear the lining of my mouth, blunt the base of my tongue, clear the way for the next bite.

Washed down with a cold glass of real orange juice, fresh-squeezed by Mama's strong hands, seeds and pulp removed with a tea strainer. And tumblers of icy milk Mama refills from a frosty jug. Sips of strong coffee, two sugars and real cream. "All I want's dry toast with my coffee," Sister whines. Whatever bothered me when I woke is mere memory now. I feel solid, as if my torso hardens as I eat, spine fusing into a truly supportive column. I get aggressive.

A large bowl of bubbling oatmeal, crumb-topped with brown sugar floating in a lake of cream. Not a lump in a carload of Mama's oatmeal! More milk. More coffee. A pan of sweetrolls hot from the oven, drizzled with frosting, gemmed with cherries. One, two, three. "Mama, you should open your own bakery," I say, wiping my brow with the back of my hand, dabbing my lips with my napkin. Four, five.

"I woke up with a headache," Sister says, will not drink her orange juice.

Another glass of milk, cup of coffee. I am beginning to feel . . . not full, but *whole*. "I'll be late to class, Mama."

"I hate to waste such nice rolls," she says, proposes to eat one more if I will.

"Excuse me, I need an aspirin," Sister says.

"It was lovely, *lovely*, Mama!" I kiss her goodbye, fetch my satchel, off to class. Ah, if only the day ended there! In the midst of this contentment, something's still amiss.

What? The salt that's supposed to be the savor? I have my classes to attend, research and study in the holy quiet of the library, a dissertation chapter to outline. Not enough. Whatever I lack, I seek it. All through the day.

A second breakfast immediately after my morning class. Two brown waffles aswim in imitation maple syrup, a bowl of corn flakes, pithy English muffins spread with translucent apple jelly, a sugary milkshake, two cups of bitter vending-machine coffee rendered tolerable with triple sugar and nondairy lightener.

A caramel-nougat bar drifted with peanut fragments to gnaw as I walk to the library, boxes of licorice, chocolate-covered mints, bags of malted-milk balls, packets of peanut-butter cracker sandwiches that crackle rudely as I open them in my carrel, pop them whole into my mouth, chew and swallow as I read.

Lunch a family-size pizza (mushrooms, Canadian bacon, onions, anchovies, studded in the marbled swirl of mozarella and tomato sauce, dusted with grated Parmesan and ground Cayenne). Vases of Coca-cola chilled by slushy ice, a little mountain of salad dotted with plump black olives, a sausage sandwich dripping dark sauce, bread stiff as two planks. What am I looking for?

Back to the library, sucking sour balls and hard candies until the roof of my mouth runs raw. Another class. My stomach growls. Now where?

The whole world, a void widening and deepening, filling with an ambience like dry fog. My eyes swim with print, hand cramped from note-taking on three-by-five cards. Thoughts veer out of their grooves. It's like the voice of someone I love calling telepathically to me. Like my spirit's left this body. I yearn after myself.

I lock my carrel, waddle to the elevator, descend, plod fecklessly among the campus trees where trysting couples grace the lyric shade. At the duck pond, coeds giggle and feed the raucous birds. A keener need draws me away. Some idealized Macklin cries out for release from his layered prison. An android blimp, I answer to a higher pitch. Like a pinball, I hit where I chance to land, carom, hit again, coming close to myself only in brief, animal moments.

An oily box of chicken parts, stale roll, paper cup of slaw, wolfed standing up at the drive-through counter. I bounce into a pancake house, bolt a stack of buckwheats the consistency of toweling, slathered with metallic blueberry syrup urged from a sticky pitcher, cutting the greasy aftertaste with sugared iced tea. I pause at a civic gumball machine, find eight pennies in my pocket, cram the pouches of my pillow cheeks like a greedy rodent, meander along the strip of beer bars and fast-food establishments bordering this end of the campus, cracking the gumballs, masticating out the sugar and artificial flavorings, spit the waxy cud into the gutter. Ruminative, waiting on inspiration or chance.

A paper tray of fish and chips dunked in tartar and ketchup. A superburger, more lettuce, tomato, and relish than meat, heavily salted fries, cola slush. Messy spareribs that slick my chin, coat my fingers. A triple cone, pralines-and-cream, black walnut, papaya. Foot-long Coney Island red hot. Stapled bag of salted-in-the-shell nuts, awkward to consume while walking, carrying my satchel, strewing broken husks behind me like a fat Hansel threading the hostile forest. Tube of breath lozenges to clear the tastebuds, freshen my hello kisses for Mama and Sister. I weary at last, go home to a long nap before dinner, mercy on these bones that must bear this body until it finds . . . something.

Mama outdoes herself. A roast big as a fireplace log, crisped like mahogany, juices running before the knife as I carve, laying the pink-red sheaves on the platter like shingles. New potatoes flecked with parsley, a heavy brown gravy smooth as paint.

"Was it a hard day, Stuart?" Mama asks, beaming as I crush and stir.

"I have a sour stomach," Sister says when Mama accuses her of eating no more than a sparrow. Steaming vegetables, each in its own tureen: french-cut beans, brussels sprouts, new peas tiny as buckshot, bloody beets, a spinach soufflé shot with cheddar, kernel corn yellow as the sun.

"Vegetables put sparkle in your skin, Sister. Isn't that so, Stuart?" I nod, mouth full. Mama's own butterhorn rolls, like English scones, buttered, folded like books, one ritual chew, melting as they're swallowed. Cold milk!

"It's hot in here," Sister says. "I lose my appetite when I get all hot."

"At least eat your nice fruit," Mama says. Glazed peach slices, plums that collapse on their pits against my gums. Baked apple. Seedless grapes. Oh! I *almost* feel I have found and quieted my lingering pain, filled that elusive emptiness echoing in me. What more?

"Surprise!" Mama cries, carrying a black-bottom pie from the kitchen.

"I don't feel like dessert," Sister says.

I resume my studies on the cleared table while Sister helps Mama with the dishes. I lose myself again, for a time, in fact and analysis, reach to dip handsful of chips or cashews from the dish Mama sends Sister to place at my dimpled elbow. Mama enjoys network television. Sister plays her bedroom stereo. Late to bed.

"Goodnight, Mama."

"Sweet dreams, Stuart."

"Night-night, Sister."

"I'll play my records soft so they won't bother you, Stuart."

I sleep. But often wake after a short time, rise, creep to the kitchen, torn again, this eternal cleft in my being. What's wrong? I arrange a snack, cold roast beef eaten with my fingers, a pint of ice cream, another slice of heavy pie. Sister and Mama sleep a peaceful sleep. I launch the thought of my trembling love for them, return to bed. I fall asleep hoping I will not dream. That I won't remember my dreams in the morning. I point my mind toward tomorrow, where I must believe I'll find myself. Where I wait for myself in mufti, some new, different, *whole* person.

Matter is not continuous; it cannot be subdivided without limit

Professor Stocker, Ph.D., is taller than me, weighs less than a third what I do. Lean as a whip, hard as a bone, dry as sandstone. "Macklin," says he, "you looking for someone to bullshit you? I crap you no crap about will power, motivation, goal orientation, positive goal ideals." We laugh. I laugh. He pulls back his lips, shows small, even, very sharp-looking teeth. Says he, "I'm *not* your friend, your father confessor. My shoulders look like they're made to cry on?" He shrugs; the white lab coat moves, the man inside unbudged.

"I get your drift."

"No you don't," he says, and, "Let's understand each other."

"The nurse explained—" I try to say, not allowed to finish. I'm in the presence of a man with convictions.

"*You* are the chief witness for the prosecution against you!" He points his finger, shakes it under my nose. "Look at you! Just look. You're a goddamn monument to unbridled self-indulgence, a living testament to weakness of spirit and absence of will, a consistent failure of human resolve!"

"I've tried," I try to say.

"You've done nothing but make yourself into a mountain of

disgusting fat from the day you were old enough to know right from wrong! You've chewed and swallowed your way through every available morsel of nutritionally destructive gunk since you lost your milk teeth!"

"It's not easy," I interrupt. Ignored.

"Why?" His voice lightens, softens. "I'll *tell* you *why!*" he thunders, retracting his finger to make a fist. "Macklin!" he says, like spitting, "Oh, I can see you clear as if I was there. You, Macklin, force-feeding your emotions until they choke to death. Plastering over every little hurt, any possibility of difficulty, burying your problems under an avalanche of food. Self, self, *self!*"

"Insults aren't hard," I say, discover I'm crying.

"I wouldn't *begin* to excuse you. Not a bit of it," Professor Stocker says. "The guilt goes just one way." He stabs at me with his rigid finger. "It's as enormous and ugly as you are. You yourself, none other." I can't stop crying.

"You think I'm hard. You think I'm hard? Okay, I'm hard on you." I shake my head, unable to speak for crying. "If I'm hard it's in context of knowing your suffering, Macklin. Macklin, are you listening to me?" I nod.

He says, "I'm not inhumane, you know. I appreciate your pain. Empathize with you. I'm the expert in this, remember? Let's begin by forgetting the obvious documented damage to your health. Heart, lungs, circulation, kidneys, liver, we assume all that, right? You think I can't imagine your subjective agony just as well? Macklin?"

"I hear you. I'm listening."

"I positively *ache* for you when I think how you must wheeze for air just getting around on foot. I understand how degrading it must be to have to wear glorified flour sacks, orthopedic shoes to support your bulging ankles. Don't you think I realize the sheer psychological pain? I'm not without normal human sympathies, Macklin."

I try to smile, stop my tears. He passes me a box of kleenex from his cluttered desk.

"And what other people must think of you when they see you,

huh? Huh? *That* smarts, doesn't it. Sure it does. Outside your family, do you suppose there's a single human being lays eyes on you doesn't experience something of the same fear and repulsion we all get when we confront a freak, a Mongoloid, say, some drooling half-wit? Ever avert your eyes from a blind man? Sure you did. Know how he'd feel if he could see it too, don't you. No I don't ignore your suffering, Macklin."

"It's why I'm here," I manage to say. I wipe my smeared face with his kleenex, cough, swallow, sniff.

"*Now* you're talking, Macklin!" says Professor Stocker, Ph.D. "Because we're going to do something about it, me and you, aren't we. Aren't we? You bet we are. Aren't we?"

"I'm willing."

"That's all I need. You stick with me, stick with the program, we can't fail. Because I've stripped it down to the bare facts of science, Macklin. You're an educated young man, Nothing succeeds like reality, and"—he lays his hand on the small refrigerator set against the wall behind his desk—"*I'm* the man discovered it, refined it, put it in a bottle for people just like you."

"I've been on reducing pills before." He laughs. We laugh. The points of his teeth flash.

"Amphetamines?" He laughs again. "I'm an associate professor, Macklin, not a drug pusher. This is *science*. I'm working on the nitty-gritty of basic human nutrition. My hypothesis functions at cell level, see? It's already done on paper. You want figures? Go over my credentials with an impartial observer?"

"I'll take your word for it."

"You won't need to," he snaps. "By Day Three, Day Five at the latest, you'll feel it happening inside you. Day Thirty, anyone you ask will tell you they see it. Day One Hundred, your own mother won't know you. You, me, and my little amino-acid compound miracle in a glass, Macklin. Game?" He takes hold of my arm. "What alternatives do you have left, Macklin?"

"You're hurting my arm!" I'm convinced. He's surprisingly strong.

You are what you eat

"I thought Professor Stocker would be here."

"Sit right there, Mr. Macklin," says Ms. Heideman, R.N., and, "Professor was called away." She goes to the motel-size refrigerator, takes a key from her pocket, unlocks the plain padlock, frees the hasp, opens the door. It has a light, like any refrigerator.

"The condemned man ate a hearty meal," I say. We neither smile nor laugh.

The amino compound is cloudy, dense, like an unset gelatin in the sealed beaker she places with a drinking glass on the professor's desk. "Is that *all* for me?"

"There's extra," says she, "should we need it." Now she has a kidney-shaped enamel pan in her hands. "You're going to find the odor strange at first, Mr. Macklin," Ms. Heideman, R.N., says. "Probably quite unpleasant." One hand goes out to the beaker, fingers resting on the rubber seal. She speaks without looking me in the eye; something's wrong.

"Professor Stocker didn't say—"

"I suggest you try and not breathe," she says as though I haven't spoken. "You know taste is strongly connected with smell. There's no aftertaste at all. Hold this under your chin," hands me the enamel pan.

"Professor Stocker should have warned me if—" She won't hear.

"If you can manage with one hand, you might try pinching your nostrils shut." Ms. Heideman, R.N., begins to inhale-exhale like a skindiver gulping air for a long descent, clamps her lips shut, cheeks distended, closes her nose with the thumb and forefinger of her left hand. With her right, she skillfully pops off the beaker's rubber lid, quickly pours exactly half the amino compound into the waiting glass, sets the beaker down, snaps the sealing lid back in place, lifts the glass to my mouth.

I have never smelled anything like it. Total. The smell is *total*. The instant the lid's off, something horrible is everywhere in the professor's office. The smell comes from everywhere, out of the paint on the walls, through the closed window overlooking the campus greensward, up from the scaling floor tiles, from Ms. Heideman's immaculate white uniform, the paper hospital gown

I wear over my shorts, oozing from the corners of my misting eyes, inside my nose and open mouth. My tears run freely. What's left after three days of hard fasting gathers, lurches for exit in my stomach. The smell's an electronic buzzing in the room, a pale fog, a sudden increase in air pressure.

I don't breathe, squeeze my brimming eyes shut, bite my lips. Ms. Heideman nudges my chin with the rim of the glass. I fear I'll drop the pan I hold to my chest. I'm afraid I'll fall out of the chair. "Drink it *fast* Mr. Macklin!" I hear her say through the smell. I can't open my mouth. "Drink!" Her voice resonates, as if from a great distance. "I said: drink!" I feel her fingers grip my hair, tip my head back. The rim of the glass clacks on my teeth. I open, swallow, gag. Swallow, swallow, gag, cough, swallow. I catch breath through my mouth. She pours the amino acid. I swallow. Swallow again.

I breathe freely, hard, blow like a walrus, paper gown pasted to me with heavy sweat. Ms. Heideman, R.N., is smiling as I opened my filmed eyes. "Are we going to keep it on our stomach, Mr. Macklin?" Hard to find enough air to speak.

"He should have told me," I sputter. "He should have said."

"Nonsense," says Ms. Heideman, R.N. There's no aftertaste. My teeth, tongue, lips feel cleansed. I can't remember what it smelled like.

"You should warn people."

"I'm proud of you, Mr. Macklin. Some of them just will not keep it down." She takes the pan from me. "I've seen a young woman won't even stay in the chair. If I had my way we'd lock the door and sit on them until they did it."

"It's the worst thing I ever had to do in my whole life," I say.

"Oh ho!" she snorts. "Life's *full* of surprises, Mr. Macklin! If you ask me, we can do just about anything we set our minds to."

In her anteoffice, she gives me four worn dollar bills; I'd forgotten the project paid participants. "It's not worth it for twenty dollars a day," I say.

"Save it in a special bank account. Think what you'll have when you're done," says she. Her mood infects me. I'm amazed, leaving, warm money folded in my hand. How good I feel. Light, alert, yet as if I'd just finished a complete, balanced meal. Professor Stocker's miracle acid!

Ecto, Endo, Meso

The world's populated by more types than meet the casual eye. My perceptions, swallowing Stocker's amino compound, weighing and measuring my shrinking hulk daily, are sharper and more profound.

Mama, for example, and Ms. Heideman, R.N. Two of a kind? Wrong. Night and day. Long and short. Thick and thin.

About the same height. When Mama presses me to her in a hug—it seems only yesterday her arms couldn't span even half my waist—my nose rests in the homey fragrance of her hair. Honest accumulation of her early old age, swaths of silver-grey, broader and deeper recently. Mama gets smaller, more frail somehow, while I, dissolving in the physiological miracle of the professor's acid seem to grow faster and faster as I measure myself against her.

No taller, Ms. Heideman awes me with her command, a sort of metaphorical superiority in size. We walk in step to the scale each day. I'm leery of the starched point of her nurse's cap, expect a poke in the eye if I dawdle. Though I've lost only a third of the weight projected for the program, I'm still a toddler next to her, dragged to a humiliating experience by a stern guardian.

Two women, approximate ages, same height, not five pounds difference between them. Same type? Wrong. No more sisters than the possum and the armadillo.

Mama's soft. A lumpy rag-bag of a woman, all sag and give, caring and comfort. Slow and sure about our home, housecoated, bathrobed, nightgowned. Cooking my breakfast—seems only yesterday—laying the dinner table, rustling a treat for late evening, casual snacks readied in the refrigerator for my insomnia. Mama's . . . *large*. But her presence soothes. Quiet without becoming moody. I close my eyes, call her up in imagination. Her gentle voice, the plop and pad of her terrycloth slippers on the kitchen linoleum. An easy mass, my Mama, relaxing as a tepid bath. I love her so!

Ms. Heideman. Density to be reckoned with. Armored in the starch of her white uniform, slashing with the blades of her cap as she marches, wheels, charges on hard legs cased in white supportive hose, big feet in square-toed white shoes, rubber heels that squeal on the anteoffice floor as if it cried out in pain at her weight. She doesn't need to touch me. Voice like a gun. "Step in the cubicle, Mr. Macklin, the gown's on the hook right inside."

"Could you maybe find me one sometime a little larger I can tie closed all the way in back?"

She says, "There'll come the day two of you can fit inside with room to swing a cat." Her conviction lends authority to the professor's calculations. Escorting me to the scale, swaying cap menacing my eye, cheek, blush-reddened ear, her sybillant stockings cheerfully hiss my seminude docility.

Everything's context. Mama, the dim, half-shabby ease of our parlor, meals baked, boiled, fried, the shuddering chug of old plumbing. Ms. Heideman, R.N., melds with the solid clank of the scale's weights, the flash of vertigo I feel as I step on the floating platform that ticks and clangs to strained stasis. Mama's hands are pale and puffy, nails dull and short. Ms. Heideman's rodlike finger worries counterweights into place, no rings, but long tapered nails glossed a stark scarlet. "Hold steady," she growls as she checks twice, enters the wonderful numbers on her clipboard.

Types. Mama, memory of caloric cloudbursts pouring forth to sustain me; Ms. Heideman an ineffable stink of amino-acid compound that, once the suffering's over, wholly satisfies.

Sister and Professor Stocker are both thin as rakes. Here, context lies in causes, not effects.

If she were only more animated, Sister might be called . . . *willowy*? She loves me very much. I love her. She's my sister.

"I'm home, Sister!" I shout. I think it cheers her. I wish the enthusiasm I lard into my voice could carry to her in the air, nourish her. Mama's hello hug and kiss, then to her bedroom. "How are you feeling today, Sister? *Okay*. Or *All right I guess*. Or *It's sort of boring*, or, the limit of her feeble spirit, *Listen to my new record, Stuart*. The pathos of her voice's delicate piping. Sick, malingering, who can say? Poor Sister. The music of third-rate crooners. Poor Sister.

She's blond, like Papa was, but her hair's lifeless, too infrequently washed. Skin so pale, spidery networks of veins show at her temples, wrists, the backs of her bony knees. So slender. Wretched posture, stoops when she stands, slumps in chairs, collapses on her bed, stares long minutes at dust motes floating in sunbeams from her window, listening—does she really *hear*—to her treasured songs of unrequited love and early death.

Mouth small, lips narrow and colorless. Blue eyes, like the professor's, but nothing in or behind to light my poor sister. Like cheap tinted glass, like a photo of a wide-eyed cadaver I once saw in a tabloid. Cause?

My metaphor's a parasite. Some tapeworm variant lodged in the wall of her gut, feeding on her embryonic emotions. Rare leech swimming in her blood, excreting only a thin fluid byproduct for her heart's need. Science won't find it. What happens when Mama dies? If I fail to come home to break the scented miasma of music she's smothering in? I refuse to think of it. A type.

Professor Stocker, Ph.D., boasts not a shred more flesh on his bones than she. But his flesh isn't flesh. Something once flesh, now fused to his skeleton by fires raging in him. A type: charred hard by the heat of his resolve.

"Don't whine," he says.

"I didn't say I couldn't," I apologize, "I just said I wasn't sure. I'd like to see you drink it sometime." As my success accelerates, I grow more assertive. Positive side-effects.

"Teach your granny to suck eggs," says Professor Stocker. Pointless to oppose him. Blue fire roars in his eyes. Flash, dance, explode. "Walk a mile in *my* shoes," says he. "You been around academe, so don't come off like you're still cherry, Macklin."

Certainly past fifty, iron-gray, coarse, tight curls, his hair catches steely highlights from the office window. Skin's a natural tan, rosied at the cheekbones and the point of his chin, color of fire behind isinglass. Thin lips almost cosmetically red. Straight nose, flared nostrils, jutting adam's apple, corded throat, tuft of grizzled hair just above the first button of his lab coat.

"Everyone has his own problems," I venture. It only turns up his burner.

"Bullshit! Macklin, you young snot. I'm solving your problem, glass by glass. Don't you dare *think* of pooping out on me! You the only man in the universe with needs? Hardy har har. I'll tell you *needs*, Mrs. Macklin's fat boy Stuart. I'm paid, you're paid, Heideman's paid, the whole shooting match's paid"—he sweeps the vista of the room with his hand, knotted with strong veins— "by a piddling seed-money grant out of a contingency fund a bitch of a lady dean squats on. For Christ's sakes, Macklin, I'm College of Home Economics faculty!" A wind blows over the blaze, fans it higher.

"I never said I wouldn't—" Futile.

"Fat-ass Macklin, know what academic tenure is? Know how you glom science-foundation grants? Know who my competition is? No. Lard-o Macklin's hungry for a doughnut and the mean professor's amino compound gives him a sore tummy!" I say no more. Know better than to stick my hand into a fire. He speaks without unclenching his teeth.

"I *need* this project, Macklin." Like a boiler approaching the red line on the gauge. "I need you and two dozen-odd more tubs signed on for four bucks a day and all the miracle stinky juice you can stand. I'm out to win, Stuart Macklin. I'm up against review committees packed with twats, fem-libbers riding high on federal equal-opportunity legislation, see? I mean to be ruthless." He pauses. Banks the fire, adjusts the draft for a bitter cold night. "Agreed?"

He waits for an answer. I perceive it as a matter of types. I'd follow him over hot coals.

A monkey in silk is still a monkey

"A man," says the grandfatherly chief salesman of Collegiate Man's Clothiers, "can't have too many clothes."

"What I'm basically doing is getting started on a wardrobe. I haven't bought anything new for a good while."

"I understand. I understand," says he. An inspiration just to look at him. Cream-white hair, full as meringue on a chiffon pie, swirled in frozen, natural whorls. The full-length triple mirror allows me to pretend to look at the suit he adjusts, smooths on me with easy, languid strokes as I watch him. "There," he says, rolling, chalking the cuffs. His words come wrapped in a secure, elderly voice, ridden by unselfconscious sighs, a tin whistle of exertion after kneeling, rising. Forty pounds overweight, at least. But at his age, on him, an appropriate padding. "How does that strike the eye, Mr. Macklin?"

Three new Stuart Macklins return my open-mouthed awe. The suit, complete with vest, is bright yellow; I glow like I've been plugged in. "I never exactly pictured myself this way. If you know what I mean."

"Of *course* I do." His smile will warm his descendants to the fifth generation. Together in the mirrors, we're a brilliant brace of triplets. Me. Macklin, a brassy, lean canary, chest swelling to sing. The canary's adopted grandfather, an immaculate owl. "The nice thing about sumptuary laws, Mr. Macklin," he says, "is that every man has a vote."

"I look good, don't I." I pirouette the three of me in the mirrors.

"You look *great*," he corrects. He'd know. Under the choreographed display of his crowning glory, his paternal eyes twinkle behind rimless spectacles with thin gold bows. *His* suit's a deep gray double-breasted, teased by a barely perceptible white thread. The pleated ascot at his throat matches the folded kerchief peeking over the slit of his breast pocket. "May I say something personal, Mr. Macklin?"

"Please do."

"I've been a member of this profession for forty years. I operated my own establishment for years. I keep my hand in here for the sheer joy." He waves graciously at the arranged lushness of

Collegiate Man's Clothiers. He wears a gold digital wristwatch, thick as a hot-rise biscuit, huge turquoise ring that would be gaudy on a less dignified man's knuckle. "I have an abiding love of things sartorial," says he.

"I never paid much attention to what I wore." I lie. Remember Mama taking me downtown on the bus each fall for back-to-school clothes bought at the Husky Boys counter in department stores. Going over illustrations in mail-order catalogues for coveralls and union suits. Shopping bargain sales at the Big Man's Store. So I lied, so what?

"You," says my adoptive grandfather, "of *all* people, should, if you'll permit me to say so." I do. His smile's a spring zephyr in the serious hush of Collegiate Man's Clothiers.

We, the two of us side by side, the six of us in the mirrors, create something. A loci. The establishment radiates from us. Long racks of suits and shirts, blocky piles of slacks on low display tables, bins of socks, neckties, underwear, tiers of shoes, poles dangling belts, glass cases of pins, links, clusters of cologne and after-shave in faceted bottles, discreetly gleaming chromed caps. The wainscotted walls and the carpet's long nap diffuse the speech of other clerks and customers to a pleasing, subservient mumble. The air's spiced, tasty with burnished leather. On the back of my tongue, I roll the flavor of motes given off by costly fabrics.

"Now, I've never said clothes *make* the man," he shakes his head, gently intolerant of this basic fallacy. "Oh my no. What I say is: men can make *themselves* by a judicious choice of attire. Look at you." We do, two observing six. "There are men who allocate a *considerable* portion of their discretionary incomes to apparel, Mr. Macklin." He squints wisely.

"I can believe it."

"Consider our clientele." His hands form them from thin air and self-assurance, to the last detail. "Occupants of endowed chairs, department heads, deans, the university president himself." What, I wonder, does Stocker wear under his lab coat? "Young gentlemen in the better social fraternities, some from families whose names are synonymous with giant corporations you would recognize instantly." His sincerity renders examples moot. His voice falls to a tone just above conspiracy. "This is the horse's mouth," he says, revealing gold inlays.

"A man such as yourself, Mr. Macklin, has an *obligation* to dress well." I understand. "You have the shoulders and chest for it, broad, masculine without being beefy. Your waist tapers without reminding people of a ballerina or a flamenco dancer. Has anyone ever told you your legs are perfectly proportioned in length to your trunk?"

"Never."

"Perhaps they didn't know." Taps his frothy sideburn with a buffed fingernail. "*I* know."

"I believe you." I do. Proof. He, me, all eight of us, self-evident.

"May I suggest," says the chief salesman, "one of our convenient accounts?"

Clutching crisp bundles, cleaner's bag over my shoulder, I stop outside. In the tinted display windows, decapitated mannequins in coats, jackets, blazers, shirts. My image among them is distinguishable only by the jaunty salute I throw myself, the candidly smug leer it evokes.

In addition to a sensible diet and adequate rest and relaxation, our good health requires that we develop a daily routine of at least moderately strenuous physical exercise

Gargantua's Disco looks like an abandoned warehouse. The pink stucco exterior is faded, cracked, pocked with chips exposing lathes underneath, windows boarded over. The name's superimposed across the dome-like belly of a gorilla painted by an amateur. Three go-go girls execute high kicks in a halo around the gorilla's head. The go-go girls are drawn out of proportion, legs at least a third too long for their orange torsos. The only light seeps out the doors when students enter. The music spills out the doors with the pale light, splattering on the street like the contents of a slop pail emptied whenever they threaten the brim. Half a block from the campus, the music's live, cover charge only two dollars. You bring in your own bottle or dope if you don't like beer.

Variety! Cream-gold sorority girls, like sets of triplets, quads, quints, so bubbling luscious I salivate. Bra-less wraiths in tee shirts, shabby jeans, sandals, bad skin and lank hair particularly unwholesome in the sickly light of the opened doors. Straight coeds with straight dates, wearing dresses, holding hands or clinging to one another's waists like shipwrecked sailors. Plug-uglies stained by acne, and, of course, fatties in clots of three and four, laughing hard to stifle their self-consciousness. If they played her music, even Sister might feel at ease in Gargantua's.

Males equally varied. Frat rats in sweaters and slacks, white shirts open at the collar, sculptured hair. Exhibitionistic dopers with frightwig Afros, obligatory jeans, embroidered chambray shirts, poor posture and furtive glances. Nondescripts in sweat-shirts, straights in blazers, suits. Turned out in my canary Collegiate Man ensemble, I'm not conspicuous.

Entering, the illusion's one of light, but the light's a plain fix-ture in the ceiling of a corridor no larger than a closet. Sound, noise. Music magnifies light. Amplified guitars and drums slam your ears, hit you like blows in a pillow fight. You're momen-tarily numbed. Someone slouching against the grimy wall plucks the two dollars I hold out, stamps the back of my hand with a purple gorilla.

Through a slashed curtain, stand as if snowblind in darkness lit by flashing strobes, buried under the music convulsing from a low stage at the deep end of the barnlike room, a rock group, Instant Gratification in foot-high gilt letters suspended from the rafters above their narcotically nodding heads.

Strobes transform the dancers to jerky stick-figures, a slide strip catching on the projector's feeder ratchets. The musical bombardment never stops. Your ears defend you, filter it down to remoteness, until Instant Gratification's lead singer even pierces their electric wailing with only occasionally intelligible words: *baby, high, love, you, me*. Your eyes withdraw.

Soon I can sort particulars, hear my thoughts clearer than anything else. The air reeks of flushed skin, textured strata of cigarette smoke edged with the dry tang of marijuana. Crowded. Everyone's alone.

Dancers a minority. Beginning with partners, most fall to private planes and spheres, wiggling in place like burlesque novices, like sexually precocious demented children, acolytes of St. Vitus. A few pass into quasimystic self-preoccupation, eyes closed, mouths open, expressionless, moving without reference to the monomaniacal rhythms of Instant Gratification. A few females shake breasts, roll buttocks as though a prurient applause were possible. The ugliest of the uglies bump, grind, thrust as if music and flashing strobes sea-changed them to voluptuousness. I watch, am bored, quit.

Nondancers are almost a tableau. Some drink beer served by humanoid bartenders in white shirts with Colonel's neckties, Fu Manchu moustaches. Some swig from bottles they grip between their knees like aged winos. A few couples sit close enough to fondle and kiss as freely as if they were locked in motels. Many look asleep, hibernating. Dopers shiver and weave. A boy shuffles past me, like some harmless asylum inmate with grounds privilege he exercises without purpose. A girl flounces past, fluid as a prostitute cruising a deserted park.

"Hello!" She hears something, not sure what. Stops. I reach, touch her bare arm. She turns, very slowly. "Hello I said." She steps closer, examines me as if I were some message scratched in crude cipher, scarcely intended for her. "Hello," I repeat, exaggerating my lips, as though I spoke with a foreigner, the hearing deficient, the mildly senile. "My name's Macklin."

"I don't know you," she says. Plain face, but the body's nature's bounty. I'm tempted to wave a finger under her nose, see if she blinks or can focus her pupils.

"Macklin," I say.

"Do I know you from somewhere?"

"It's hard to talk in this noise." She turns her head a little to see what I'm talking about.

"You want to go outside?" She speaks to me as if I were a contrary child left in her care.

"Whatever you want." She looks at me—hard to say how long

when time is so vague, where no one has reference to anything, anyone else. Takes my hand, leads me through the frozen crush to the exit, past the doorkeeper, head down on his chest. Leads me by the hand like a mother seeking a comfort station for her incontinent toddler.

Outside. Like waking suddenly from a dream so grotesque you dare have no slightest memory of it, fresh air banishing terror. The music, like excruciating pain, cannot be recalled. Ordinary dark of night, like the playful splash of cool water. Leads me down the street, around the corner. Houses, lawns, grass, and trees. A van with opaque bubble windows, panels painted with forest and mountain panoramas. Opens the rear door, crawls in ahead without releasing my hand. Her hand is dry, mine slippery. I crouch, enter. The rasp of carpeting everywhere, polished fittings and fixtures. She sits Indian-fashion.

"You're cute," she says. "Do you want to smoke or ball?"

"I don't need any dope," I say. Help her out of her jeans.

"Leave it on," she says when I try to pull her jersey over her head.

"Relax your arm, it'll slip right off," I say, surprised how calm my voice is.

"No! If I smear the stamp off I can't get back in without paying again." All the while, she holds her stamped hand aloft, as if she stroked an invisible wellwisher who watched us. "What are you doing?" she asks.

"This suit's brand new," I say, carefully folding my jacket and trousers, laying them softly with my vest, out of range behind me. I did not even consider, seriously, telling her she had the distinction of my virginity.

We are such stuff as dreams are made on

Where's Ms. Heideman? For a moment I thought the ante-office was locked, no light diffusing through the opaque glass pane in the door, no clicking typewriter keys, file drawer ramming home, floor protesting her shoes. But the knob turns in my hand. "Ms. Heideman?" Dim, empty, no echo to my voice.

Swept clean. No desk, no chair, no plastic-covered couch for waiting, no files, telephone, file folders, in-out tray. The scale still stood in the hallway, but the dressing screen was folded, propped against the wall. Stocker's door opened too, and I found him there, sitting at his desk, illuminated only by the window overlooking the campus greensward.

"When I saw she was gone I figured you'd be gone too," I say. And when he doesn't speak, "It's me, Macklin."

"Do tell," says Professor Stocker. "Mrs. Macklin's former fat boy, come to show off his fancy duds, let us all bask in his new glory. How far'd you chase that nigger for his suit?"

"I haven't seen you in so long," I say. "I just wanted to say thanks for all you did for me." I'm not sure he's listening.

"Go away, Macklin," Stocker says. "See the door? Pull it to you and run. Don't let the knob hit you in the ass. Go. The project's over. The till's dry if you're looking to cadge four bucks. Magic juice's all dried. Leave me to hell alone, Macklin."

"What is it with you?" His desk's cleared too. The examination table still there, and the refrigerator, plug pulled. "I thought you'd be glad to see me."

"Macklin," the professor says, "come to gloat over his new self. Okay. You're a marvel to behold. Broads falling back over their heels for you, are they? So gloat. Have a good life, Macklin." His voice. The way he sits. Nothing in his voice but words. Sitting I wonder how long with the light off, speaking like an old recording, ashes and cinders.

"I don't get it. I thought you'd be happy. It worked, right? Look at me! Living proof." He laughs like it was an accident happened to someone he hated.

"Macklin," he says, throws back his head, tilts back in his swivel chair, speaks like he reads print on the ceiling. "The widow Mrs. Macklin's fat boy. A sister, too, right? I remember him well. Pushing five hundred avoirdupois, one big ball of adipose. Cellulite to the bone, weren't you. Decked out now like a dancing fag. Oh, Jesus."

"It's probably not good for you to sit all by yourself here."

"The man just does *not* twig!" He tilts forward, looks at me. I step to where I can see his eyes. What's left, cold and dry. "The exception proves the rule, see? Get it? I failed, Macklin. El bombo. Funds expended and accounted for. Done. Dr. Stocker's amino-acid compound hypothesis went bust, see? Go away."

"It *did* work! Look at me. The other—"

"Dunce," says he, "there ain't no *others*! Start with thirty-seven volunteers. Prize fatties. Blimps. Tubbies all. Half can't fast long enough to start. Half the rest, Heideman couldn't scare them into the first drink. You wouldn't blame them for barfing at the smell, would you? Half what's left never held a dose down. Make a guess how many times Heideman had to change her clothes. Get it? Three of you. Three came back for a second taste, Macklin. One besides you made it past the first week. You ninny, I knew from the second week it was a bust! Doctoral candidate in quant analysis doesn't know what an adequate sample is? Get lost, Macklin."

"Why'd you keep me, then? Tell me."

"Just wanted to see if you could. Sheer-ass curiosity. I got interested," the professor says. "Involved. Enjoy yourself, Macklin. Watch that maintenance diet, though, that lard'll come back on you like stink on shit."

"At least I came to say thanks, even considering I'm the one did the hard part."

"Think of me sometimes, Macklin," he says.

I should say goodbye, something special in appreciation for his helping me do it. But he doesn't want to listen. Nobody should blame him for the ones who dropped out. And the real credit's mine for me. I've got enough responsibility for myself. Nothing's easy. I say: if you got it, flaunt it. I'd like to tell him, complaining never cut a single calorie.

The bigger the figure, the better I like 'em,
The better I like 'em, the better I feed 'em,
The better I feed 'em, the bigger the figure,
The bigger the figure, the better I like!

"I'll be late, Mama." Wipe my mouth with the back of my hand. Anyone thinks a brewer's yeast cocktail's rough never tried amino acid.

"You can't live like this," Mama says. She stands midway between the sink and the stove. The table's set for the three of us, plates, silver, cups and saucers, juice glasses, but the stove's cold, percolator unplugged. I set my satchel on the floor. I don't seek this.

"Yes I can. I am. Look at me. I never felt better." I go to kiss her goodbye, but she flinches.

"Crazy," she says. "You're making us all crazy with this. You have to eat sensibly now, even your crazy professor said so. I can cook anything you want. Nobody can live this way." Mama crying. When Papa died she didn't cry until his funeral. After, late at night when she thought I was asleep, I always got up, went to her, hugged and kissed. She'd dry her eyes, make us a snack, tuck me in again, whispering not to wake Sister, just a baby then.

"Stop it." She does. "That's not fair. You can't do that to me anymore. Don't ever do that again." She comes to me, puts her arms around me, hands crossed behind my back. Odd. Me so thin, yet she seems so much smaller now. We say nothing, hear only Sister's radio-alarm begin to play. "Sister's going to come out in a minute," I say. At first I think she's sobbing again—she'll get my new shirt wet! But she's talking, muffled against my chest.

"Won't you talk to me? Oh won't you talk to me, Stuart?" She lifts her head, looks at me with runny eyes. "I can't talk to my boy. My boy won't tell me what's the matter. It's making me go crazy." She releases me before I ask her to. I step away.

"That's stupid. You just can't accept what I've done. How do you think it makes me feel? I need to be disciplined. You think my maintenance diet's fun? You should be pleased for me. Look!" I half-turn, arms extended, half-dance for her in our kitchen, hop, kick my heels in midair.

When I see Sister in the doorway, leaning slackly against the frame, wrapped in her robe, feet bare, hair tangled from sleep. I freeze, almost fall. "Stuart," Mama says.

"I got to run," I say. "Goodbye, Mama. Bye, Sister," leave before they can answer. Later in the day, sitting in my carrel, I remember I failed to hug and kiss. I promise to give them double when I get home. That, I know, will just cause more trouble.

Evening. I read in my bedroom while they eat dinner. In the kitchen. No point in laying the dining-room table if we're not going to sit down like a family, Mama says. "It's crazy for me and Sister to sit eating while you bury your nose in a book," she says.

"Eat your supper, you two," I tell them, "You won't even know I'm alive."

I'm more efficient than ever. Mind keener, retaining more. Like amphetamines or a fasting high. I concentrate. A kind of power. Can't help gloating. No doubt Professor Stocker could explain it scientifically, sound mind in a sound body. No need.

My own metaphor suffices. My new self's uncluttered, unchained, minus over three hundred pounds of fatty tissue. Free. I'm cleaner, lighter, simpler, more exact with each day I hold to my maintenance program. More than physical. Sure, heart beating easier, less rapidly, blood coursing a shorter distance to my extremities, lungs gleaning more oxygen, distributing it more evenly and generously. More than that. *Found*. Myself. What I looked for, eating, all my life. The *real* Macklin. *Macklin*, I say to myself, smack my lips like it was a vitamin-enriched confection. *Macklin!* I snigger to myself over my book, in my bedroom, alone.

"Stuart?" Mama says at my door.

"I'm studying."

"There's a good show on TV."

"I *said* I was studying."

She goes away. Silence. I forget them, the house, the television murmur I could hear if I wanted. Forget. Except Macklin. Me. Him, emerging day by day, finer definition, larger as he's smaller. Greater for being less. What he sees, hears, smells. Words he reads, gaining without adding the least fraction of an ounce. Macklin. *Macklin*, I say, lipping the initial consonant, gulping the vowel, tonguing the close against my teeth, swallowing.

"Are you going out, Stuart?"

"Would I wear a new suit if I wasn't?" Powder blue so posh you could eat it with a spoon.

"Stuart's got a heavy date," Sister sneers.

"Would you like to go along with him, Sister?" Mama says.

"Hey! Did I invite company?" I say. I should leave on that. Why prolong an agony? "Macklin's had a bad day," I say to them. "Classes, working in the library. He's read his eyes out half the night trying to make something of himself in this life. Do you grudge me some recreation?"

My mother begins to cry. My sister cringes into her chair. My sister is also weeping. I wait until they find enough control to stammer apologies. I'm not angry, just determined. Do, I have learned, what you must. Then what you can. Ignore the impossible.

What a night for a walk! I walk fast, almost skipping. No hard feelings. They'll get over it. Or they won't. I already have. I pick up my pace. Turn a corner, catch the feeble light, suggestion of disco music.

Mirror, Mirror, on the wall,
Who's the fairest of them all?

Reminders. Old habits persist. I work at it, water on stone, new habits for old. Smart would be, pack and leave town. Soon enough. Meantime, I accept the challenge, the long haul. I'm a man knows the value of discipline applied over a course of time. Basic dialectics: quantitative changes, past a certain point, become qualitative.

Stick to business on campus. Things go well. Finishing the dissertation, conferences with my major professor, assembling a dossier with the placement service. I run into old faces. Neither seek nor evade.

I pass the student infirmary as the lunch hour knells on the carillon. Ms. Heideman emerges, stout and hard as ever, cap squared, shoulders back, bust outthrust under her dark blue cape. Must be dull work. Runny noses and sore throats, hot streaks when a flu bug mingles with the student body. Occasional fractures from intramural sports to jar the monotony of malingerers looking for chits to excuse class absence. I neither wave nor look away. She sees me, must. No recognition. My prime witness, administered it drink by nauseating drink, measured it pound by pound on her clanking scale. I can admire her.

Given a job, does it. On to the next. I respect a plodder. Determination and accomplishment, no matter how mundane. What was, was. Now's now. We pass one another, and that's all. I'll get on fine with the Heidemans of this world.

Stocker's another story. Seen him twice recently, ambling past the duckpond. Wearing his lab coat. Of course we don't speak. It hurts, a little. A whipped dog, stooped, greatly aged in so few months. Preoccupied somewhere inside himself, uncertain, awkward. The breaks. I sleep in my bed, he in his. The way I see it: we took a shot together, mine hit, his fell short. Live and let live.

I call my mother at least once a week. No problem. "I can't make that, Mama," I tell her. "You should quit asking me."

"I can fix anything you want, Stuart," she says. "I'll special buy what you want. Your sister would like seeing you."

"You know better, Mama." You have to be firm. No pun.

"She's your sister. We're your family."

"So? Look, Mama, I have to meet somebody."

"A girl?"

"Don't ask dumb questions. Listen, take care of yourself. Tell Sister for God's sake to get out of the house once in a blue moon."

"You have to make allowances for other people, Stuart."

"No," I say. Say goodbye. I call regularly.

Hanging tough. Whiff of hot cooking oil, TV commercial for doughnuts, billboard featuring a cross-sectioned candy bar. I confess to automatic reactions. Spontaneous salivation, harsh winces of the stomach. My fingers clench into fists, palms sweat, breath comes short and fast. Children pass, licking popsicles. A grocery clerk anoints fresh produce with a spray bottle. A bakery truck rumbles by. Fast-food personalities flash plastic grins at me. I set my teeth, narrow my eyes, break into a trot. Prepared to cope with my glands the rest of my life, the long haul, if I must.

Truly strange, what I call my . . . *visions*. Tricks of the imagination. Infrequent, once or twice a day. I pass a mirror, a plate-glass window, a reflective puddle of rainwater. I see . . . Macklin. Trim as a welterweight. Hard as oak siding. Macklin, able to stand inside one leg of an old pair of trousers, room for his twin left over. And I see Macklin. Before and after, testimonial for reducing formulae, a kind of double vision. Macklin half the man he was. Macklin whole.

I sense the sympathetic aura of my old body enveloping me. Feel my heart struggle, lungs heave, blood slosh feebly toward the distant limits of what was once . . . me, Macklin.

Go away, I command. Run my hands over my body, poke my taut abdomen, dig fingers into a wiry bicep, shake a racer's leg, stroke my muscular throat, shake my deflated behind. *Go away, Macklin.* He does. But returns. I look for a long haul.

Sleeping, I'm helpless. Naturally I dream of food, drink, myself at twice or three times my new weight. My dream sister pines, mother pleads, Stocker mourns, Heideman executes. Dream myself teased and scorned by easy women, dream motley wardrobes, the ineffable stench of an amino-acid compound I almost think lingers after I wake.

Overall, I accept a long haul. All in all, I'm grateful to be alive, sometimes regret my father didn't live, that I have to imagine my joy in his pride.

If a Man Truly in His Heart

There were two cars parked at the Lamar County jail when Eldon got there, Sheriff Boyd's and a state highway patrol. When he parked his patrol car next to the state car, shut the engine off, Eldon heard their radio going softly, logging a coded report of a three-death accident down toward Gulfport.

Fike McCain was standing on the front steps of the jailhouse, like Eldon needed someone to show him how to find the office. The advantage of Fike being colored, Eldon thought, was nobody expected anything from him, so he never caught hell for the nothing he did. It was enough to make a man wish he was a nigger sometimes. Like not having to speak until after someone else spoke first.

"Highway patrol catch Boyd speeding for coffee to the truck-stop?" Eldon said. What he hoped it was was the sheriff not where he was supposed to be when the state police wanted him. The idea was, Sheriff Boyd patrolled nights, which was a joke. What he did was sleep in a cell, or sit at the truck-stop having coffees with truckers, or even going home to watch the television, leaving Fike McCain to sit the jail just in case.

Eldon was the day shift. Which was a big joke, getting called out of his house trailer away from his family in the middle of the night.

"Some *bad* business this night," Fike said. He shook his head, made a sucking noise with his tongue to show how bad and serious it was.

What it was, the highway patrol had brought in a prisoner to leave overnight. Sheriff Boyd's luck was naturally good. He had been right there at his desk, playing with the radio to get CB talk from I-35, when they brought the prisoner in. Eldon did not see the prisoner right away. They had him on a chair in the corner behind them. Eldon had to deal first with them.

"Hell," one of the highway patrol said, "looks to me like you got more security in your big nigger." Sheriff Boyd gave him a big laugh for that. Fike McCain turned right around and went back outside. That was the advantage of being a nigger, you could just walk away from unpleasantness. Eldon had to stay there and figure out just how much smile he was supposed to put on his face for a joke about himself.

"He's small, but he's *mean*," the sheriff said, and Sheriff Boyd and the two highway patrol all smiled at that. Eldon did not know what to do with himself. Sheriff Boyd sat on the edge of his desk, a natural enough place for him to be, grinning like a mule chewing briars. The two highway patrol stood side by side, very straight, like they never sat down except in their patrol car, to keep from putting too many wrinkles in their uniforms.

"He better look like it if he ain't," the other highway patrol said. Eldon could not decide if he should find a spot to sit, like the sheriff, or stand up like a statue with the two highway patrol. He stood where he was, because he did not feel free to sit, did not want to be any closer to the highway patrol. They were very big men. He would feel even smaller if he stood close to them.

They were always big. You had to be a certain size to join the state police, besides knowing some politician. Eldon was under-size for it. They were always tall and heavy. Even when they got old and gone fat you could see they were not fat old men, but big men who had gone some fat just getting older. They did not smile or laugh for jokes anybody else made. If they smiled or made a joke, still Eldon could always see that under the smile was a big very serious man who did not ever really smile or laugh.

They were men he knew had true meanness in them, deep. At the bottom and heart of them was a meanness they kept for when they wanted it.

Their uniforms made them look bigger, ten-gallon hats, gold badges on their hats and on their shirts, special black plastic nametags on the pocket flap, white letters. One's nametag said *Hatcher, C. L.* The other one was *Tharpe, J.*

They carried full-sized Magnum revolvers, and their brass was always blitzed like new, the pointy toes of their cowboy boots polished hard as glass. Their gabardines were crisp and clean, the handcuffs and come-along chains they carried on their belts chromeplated, their leather buffed. They made Eldon feel the meanness at the heart of them, a meanness which let them whip a cuffed man to death with their hands and toes and high heels of their boots.

"I will be as close as my car's radio," Sheriff Boyd said.

"We brung you a real mean one," C. L. Hatcher said. Then Eldon saw the prisoner for the first time. The two highway patrol stepped apart to give him a good look at him, sitting on a chair in the corner.

"It is not I'm so bad," the prisoner said, "but that I have knowed a few boys who thought they was until I showed them different."

"Damn your smart mouth," J. Tharpe said. He did not seem to move. He just leaned toward the prisoner and slapped him open-hand. But it did not shake the prisoner, did not even ruffle his hair.

He was bigger than anybody Eldon had ever seen. He was sitting, hands cuffed in front of him, but more like he held his hands folded in his lap, like he could lift and separate his hands whenever he cared to. Sitting, he was still larger than the highway patrol. He had gone fat, but the huge man was there under the fat.

He wore only a tee-shirt and slacks, his shoulders and the roll of fat at his middle bulging out the tee-shirt. His arms were bare, covered with so many large blue-black tattoos it looked like the ink had run, been blotted, tiny flecks of color here and there among all the blue-black tattoos. His head was big and round as a cooking pot, his cheeks rosy in the bright jail office light. On his thick wrists, the handcuffs were like a lady's thin bracelets.

His feet were bare, his shoes with the plain white socks tucked into the tops next to his chair. The prisoner's feet were red and black with dried blood, where the two highway patrol had taken away his shoes after they cuffed him and stomped his feet with their boots to discourage him from thinking about running off.

"He likes to escape jails," C. L. Hatcher said.

"I have ex-caped more than one time," the prisoner said. He did not speak like he was afraid of slaps and stomping. "You would have did the same," he said.

"The famous Gary Lee Stringer," J. Tharpe said, "and we got him, C. L. and me. Come to us easy as pie. Right out on I-35, on his way to New Orleans, I reckon."

"Riding without no taillights in a damn old junk pickup," C. L. Hatcher said. J. Tharpe leaned toward the prisoner like he meant to slap him again, but did not. That was the difference between him and them, Eldon thought. I never whipped on a man was cuffed, hit him when I had him safe in my jail. Eldon would have bet wages it was J. Tharpe took away the man's shoes and stomped on his feet with his boots. J. Tharpe was a little smaller than his partner, with broken veins in his cheeks and the end of his nose, watery blue eyes that looked happy to do some meanness at any time.

Gary Lee Stringer said, "I ex-caped Parchman plantation, and Big Mac in Oklahoma, and I ex-caped the Louisiana prison farm at Angola. It is the worst of all the ones I been in."

"I calculate he's been hid in New Orleans since he run from Angola," C. L. Hatcher said.

"Gary Lee Stringer the famous criminal thief and killer," J. Tharpe said. "Where was you running to when you come to me, Gary Lee Stringer?"

Gary Lee Stringer said, "I will not identify where I been."

"He come easy," J. Tharpe said. "Maybe he only kills police officers when they got their back turned to him."

"I have seen bad actors be meek as cats," the sheriff said. Which was a joke, Eldon thought. When it was a call for some-body drunk beating his family or breaking up the truck-stop, the sheriff sent Eldon Sistrunk to bring the man to a cell.

"I was of no mind to offer you harm," Gary Lee Stringer said.

It was Gary Lee Stringer they had in the Lamar County jail. The famous killer and escape artist. His picture was right on the bulletin board in the jail office. Eldon shot his eyes to it, picked him out among all the bank robbers and fugitives from justice and military deserters the FBI furnished pictures of. His picture had been in the newspaper in Jackson, and in the paper in Hattiesburg and Gulfport and New Orleans and Memphis. He was very famous. He looked only huge, not mean or a man planning to kill or escape anywhere.

"I made certain he would not escape us once we got him cuffed," J. Tharpe said, and kicked the prisoner's bare feet with the pointy toe of his boot. Gary Lee Stringer winced, moved on the chair like he just discovered he had hurt feet. Why, Eldon thought, he is hurting like any natural man. "I'd as leave killed him for all what he's done," J. Tharpe said. The sheriff and the two highway patrol laughed at that. Eldon put a smile on his face.

"I believe the governor of Mississippi will present us personal citations for this," C. L. Hatcher said, and they all of them smiled again.

It was Gary Lee Stringer the famous killer and escape artist. He was from people up near Soso, where years back they buried killed moonshiners under their doorsteps to hide the fact from federal agents who killed them. He was from people who were pure trash, but had become famous. Eldon remembered how Gary Lee Stringer started off his life, playing football for Soso, and then a while at Ole Miss until they threw him out for what he did to some fraternity students after a game once. Then he was a star player for Mississippi Southern College, right over at Hattiesburg, when they had the famous team that was half of them former convicts from Parchman and the rest who should have been in Parchman. But it was a great team Eldon followed when he started high school in Purvis. Once they beat Alabama.

"We will get more than citations, C. L.," J. Tharpe said. "We will get our picture taken in the Jackson newspaper, and transfers. We will get out of here to Jackson or Gulfport, or maybe up near Memphis." The two highway patrol smiled at each other, and the sheriff grinned at them. Eldon did another little smile on his face.

When Gary Lee Stringer left Mississippi Southern's football team and went away to the Marine Corps, they could not hold him where he did not want to stay. He ran away from the Marine Corps to his people near Soso, Mississippi, until they came and took him back to a Marine Corps prison in South Carolina, but he escaped, the first of his famous ones. He robbed his way back to Soso again, and for a time lived quietly and got married. When at last they took him up to Parchman plantation, they could no longer hold him anywhere.

He killed a trusty guard at Parchman, and it was that way ever since. Escaping whatever jail they put him in, robbing for a living, hiding out sometimes near Soso to be with his people. Up in Tunica County he killed a deputy sheriff, and in Louisiana a highway patrol, and was sentenced to die, but escaped again. He was a famous bad and mean man. It made Eldon hold his skin tight to keep from shivering just to be in the same room with him. It was the feeling of being near someone special, like being in person with the governor of the state, or the time in the army, when he was an MP, Eldon stood honor guard for a general with four stars once.

"If he don't get a-loose from this jail tonight," C. L. Hatcher said.

"We will see to that, boys," Sheriff Boyd said. "Get the keys," he said to Fike McCain, who was suddenly back in the office with them. A nigger was like that, Eldon thought. Going and coming when he pleased, sneaking up on you, sneaking off. You could not trust them, and nothing to be done about it. To the two highway patrol, the sheriff said, "This boy Eldon Sistrunk is little, but he is a feis. He is my nephew by marriage to my niece Marice, and almost like a son to me. He'd sooner die than let us down, boys. My turnkey will keep him awake." That was a big joke for all of them, even Fike McCain shaking himself like he was biting off laughing under his breath, shaking the keyring to make it jangle with his laughing. Eldon smiled back at them. He had to say something.

"Maybe you had ought to take such a famous person right on over to Hattiesburg to be on the safe side of it," was all he could think to say. They laughed like that was a joke too.

"You do not understand getting publicity," J. Tharpe said.

"Why should my station commander get his picture in the newspaper when we's the ones captured mean Gary Stringer?" C. L. Hatcher said.

"It is sharing the wealth a little with us, Eldon," Sheriff Boyd said. They explained it to him. He had to stand there like he was slow in the mind as Fike McCain, nodding. If they took the famous criminal to the Hattiesburg station, they would just have to sign him over and go back out to finish their patrol. J. Tharpe and C. L. Hatcher would read all about it the next day. Their station commander would get all the show with the newspaper he could call for the minute he sent them back out to patrol. They would be lucky to get even their names in the paper for catching Gary Lee Stringer. This way, they would come back to Purvis and pick up their prisoner, carry him to Hattiesburg when they signed in off patrol, be the ones to call the newspaper themselves.

"I expect a picture of us with him might could be in newspapers in Memphis and New Orleans," J. Tharpe said.

"I expect these boys will give our names when they do their interviews and all," the sheriff said to Eldon. Fike McCain opened the big holding cell, the cuffs were removed, and they shoved Gary Lee Stringer in, locked the door. He went to the cot against the far wall, rubbing his wrists, sat looking out at them. "I will show you what security is," Sheriff Boyd said to the highway patrol.

He sent Fike McCain for a chair, seated Eldon facing the cell. Then the sheriff got the new riot gun purchased for the county with a federal grant, loaded it, gave it to Eldon to hold across his knees. The gun was heavy, so new it still smelled of the cosmoline pack it came in. Eldon sat on the chair with the riot gun,

squinting against the light of the bare overhead bulb, looking at
Gary Lee Stringer sitting back in the shadows of the cell, rubbing
his wrists.

"I might could be subject to get a call of nature," Gary Lee
Stringer said from his cot.

"Pan under the bed," Fike McCain said. He was always around
when you did not know it, sneaking in and out in his nigger way.
It was not fair, Eldon thought. Eldon had to be places on time,
have answers, show responsibility. He had to smile or not, de-
pending on what was wanted. Fike did not. Fike McCain was
a dumb old nigger, so all he had to do was act like one. Slow
moving, mumbling and chuckling, coming and going when it
pleased him. Everyone thought he did just fine.

"I will keep these on patrol with me," the sheriff said, taking
the keyring from Fike's hand.

"Ain't we going to feed or water him even?" was all Eldon
could think to say. They did not even trust him that much.

"If he even looks like wanting out of there, you shoot him," J.
Tharpe said. "Do it in his legs or feet. No way they can make a
newspaper picture of a dead man."

"What if the jail gets on fire?" Eldon said. "Will they show his
picture burned up since I ain't got no way to get him out?" He
kept from smiling. That was a good one he dared not let show in
his face.

"No damn fire—" Sheriff Boyd started to say.

"Leave him the keys," C. L. Hatcher said.

"No governor will shake the hand of a law enforcement officer
lets a famous criminal and escape artist get burned up to cinders
in the damn Purvis jail," J. Tharpe said. The sheriff gave him the
keys. Eldon looked for Fike, to turn them over to him to hold,
but Fike had slipped away again. He tucked the keys behind his
cartridge belt. His wife's uncle came back after seeing the highway patrol out.

"I do not at all appreciate that."

"You can take the key all the same," Eldon said.

"Don't sass me."

"Nossir," he said. Then he said more, surprising himself. "You can sit with me if you think I ain't security enough, Uncle Boyd."

The sheriff just looked at him for a minute, looked over at Gary Lee Stringer to see if he was paying attention, then said to him, "Do you think you are a deputy sheriff because you can get votes at election for me? Why do you think you are my deputy? Does my niece your wife Marice like for you to have a decent respectable job in this county? I am speaking to you, Eldon Sistrunk."

"Yessir," Eldon said.

"I have got to go patrol. That is why they choose me the sheriff for Lamar County at every election. They *know* me," his wife's uncle said. "You," he said, "are not nobody but my niece Marice's husband. *My* daddy was sheriffing this county before me. Your daddy was a trashy pulpwood cutter, worked with niggers, *like* a nigger. Don't you never forget why you are my deputy. Are you hearing me?" Sheriff Boyd said.

"I am. I think about it a lot." He looked down the corridor to see if Fike had sneaked in, but he had not.

"Best you do," the sheriff said, then left. You are all a damn lie, Eldon thought. Whipping on men is cuffed, drinking coffees in the truck-stop instead of doing patrol, playing with the CB on the car radio, getting your picture in the newspaper to be famous if you can.

"Life is nothing but a pure misery, ain't it?" Gary Lee Stringer said from the cell.

"You best *shut* your mouth!" Eldon said, and took a fresh grip on the new riot gun.

He did not know how long he had been sitting that way before the prisoner spoke again. He sat holding the gun, his back straight against the chair, squinching his eyes against the hard light of the bare bulb, pretending to see into the holding cell where Gary Lee Stringer sat on the cot as still as if his hands were still cuffed. Eldon was thinking.

His daddy had *not* been trash. He cut pulpwood for the Masonite plant in Laurel, and rented some acres to grow melons, tried a peach orchard on his own little box of land out by Black Creek where the gas-cracking plant was now. Even if his daddy was trash, Eldon knew *he* was not. He had gone to the high school in Purvis, the old one that was closed when they had the forced integration. Eldon was too small to play football. When he left school for the army, though, he was big enough to be an MP. And Marice Boyd did not think he was too small when he came home in his MP uniform. Eldon's daddy went to brush arbor meetings and tent revivals to regularly swear off moonshine, but Eldon and Marice and their three sons went each Sunday and Wednesday to hear Brother John Barnes preach Jesus at the Free Baptist Assembly of Purvis. His sons went to vacation Bible school. Eldon would have whipped them if they did not. His daddy squatted land was not his, it turned out when they came to build the Black Creek refinery, but Eldon owned his lot in the trailer park, and the trailer house would be his free and clear soon enough. In time he would sell and pay down on a ranch-style house like all the ones building up this end of the county for men working the gas-cracking plant. He was a married man and a family man and the deputy sheriff of Lamar County, Mississippi, and no man dast to call him trash like he was trash or a nigger.

"It won't rub off on you, just talking to me to pass time," Gary Lee Stringer said from his cot.

"What? I *told* you to keep hushed," Eldon said. It was like coming out of a dream, finding himself awake, sitting on the hard chair facing the cell, the heavy gun across his legs.

"Do not believe all you read in a newspaper about me," Gary Lee Stringer said. "I am only a natural man like you. I can't do you harm talking. If I was a mind to do harm, them two would of not got their hands on me for long."

Eldon made a smile on his face to show him what he thought of that. "I suppose you would of fought the both of them together."

"That is the truth in your heart you are saying," Gary Lee Stringer said.

"That is a joke," Eldon said, "You against the both."

"No it ain't. Me against two, against five don't give me pause if I don't decide it. I knowed men thought it was funny up to where I showed them. You can read it in the newspaper if you don't believe me. That part, what all I have did in my life, you can believe. What you can't is I am some sort of special breed of meanness. If you'd been from Soso instead of here, you'd known me, seen I ain't no different."

"Excepting you like to talk on," Eldon said. He was not comfortable on the chair. The shotgun was heavy across his knees, hard and sharp-cornered to the touch of his hands. He had a headache. He would call out for Fike to find the aspirin bottle in the sheriff's desk.

"When it's the truth I do," Gary Lee Stringer said.

"I prefer you sit on your bunk," Eldon said when the prisoner started to stand up. Eldon tried to listen for the sound of Fike poking around in the office, heard nothing.

"I understand it," Gary Lee Stringer said. He squirmed to settle himself back against the wall on the cot. He was almost hidden in the deep shadow. "I will go along with any man speaks the truth to me. It is liars I don't abide." His voice rose, came out of the shadow with the edge of an echo from the close walls of the cell. "It is liars made me mean from the very start."

"Don't shout," Eldon said. "You will scare off my turnkey."

"I get some carried off when I think of it all," Gary Lee Stringer said.

"Let's us be calm and quiet. It will be morning soon enough," Eldon said, "They will come take you to Hattiesburg and you be made famous some more."

He heard the prisoner sigh, heard the cot creak as he settled in, as if to doze with his head against the wall. Then they were quiet again for a long time. Eldon could not get comfortable. He half-closed his eyes against the light of the bare bulb. He tried thinking of particular things.

Marice and his sons were sleeping in their trailer home. It would be paid for in less than four years. It was a good one, anchored down against anything but a tornado. On the highest shelf in the closet was where he kept his .32 pistol when he was off duty, where his sons could not reach it. When the trailer home was paid up he would sell it and the lot he owned where it sat. He would have the downpayment for a ranch-style house where all the refinery men lived. He would be deputy to Marice's uncle until the sheriff died or retired, and then it might could be he would win his own election to sheriff. He was a good soldier, an outstanding MP in the army. He had been too small to play football, but he could handle bigger men who got drunk in road-houses and came home to beat on their family.

He thought, I have done pretty good in my life, and if I keep on I might could be a true success. He tried thinking on ahead how it might be in years to come, but there were no particulars, and his head ached from lacking sleep and having to smile and be the joke for the sheriff and having no one he could talk with. I will think only of this very exact moment. Eldon thought, but there was nothing to think about in that. He was glad when Gary Lee Stringer spoke again.

"You don't favor your uncle the sheriff any I can discern," he said.

"It is by marriage only. My wife is his dead brother's girl who used to be the deputy up until he died of a sudden stroke, is how come I am now. You can get up and walk around if it eases you," Eldon said. "You're free to stretch out and sleep too." He hoped Gary Lee Stringer would not go to sleep, leave him alone in the cell corridor with the shotgun weighing him down, nobody but Fike McCain around, out in the jail office.

He did stand up, arched his back. He was enormous, like a tree or a house. "I am not of no mind to sleep, what all I got on my mind to think over," he said.

"I will have the turnkey make us some coffee. It's too late to send him out for food," Eldon said.

"I thank you kindly, but no," Gary Lee Stringer said. "You probably think I am some big eater, big as I am." He came for-ward in the cell, put his hands on the bars. His hands were so big it looked like he could rip the bars away if he wanted. He grinned at Eldon, a real grin. "I come by my size honest. My daddy and mama both is large people, big bone and heavy. But I eat spare, the life I live. Hiding out and running," Gary Lee Stringer said, "I skip many's a meal." They laughed together.

"Me," Eldon said, "I always been small and lean. Marice says I eat like two my size, but I never gain a ounce."

"Marice is your wife," Gary Lee Stringer said like he was telling Eldon what he did not know.

"We have three boys," Eldon said. They looked directly at each other. Eldon could only look back at him, stare him out, feeling it was somehow wrong to be speaking his family's names to this man. He looked back into the prisoner's eyes, pretending to be waiting for him to speak next, hoping he would hear Fike McCain in the jail office.

"We are two men the same way," Gary Lee Stringer said. "To my mind, we are alike a lot." Eldon nodded, not sure what he meant exactly, but it felt right to hear it. "We have wives and young ones, you and me, and we love them. I can tell you love them with all your heart."

The words came to Eldon like something he had wanted to be able to say, had felt but could not find words for before now. It was like being told the sense for something that had hold of you so close you did not see it until you heard the words making it clear. "And they's the source of all our misery, too," Gary Lee Stringer said. They looked at each other, not smiling at all because there was no joke in this.

"Explain me how it is that," Eldon said.

"Because of the love," he said, "a man does all kinds of things in his life. I am the proving of that. Look in your heart, you will see it's true. It don't any of it mean a thing except a man has found somebody or something, like you and me, he loves. Then he is pained because he had did all kind of things to his life, and the loving of them makes us hurt for what we have did."

"You sound like some stump preacher," Eldon said. He almost told him to shut up. He sat still for Brother John Barnes of the Free Baptist Assembly of Purvis, Mississippi, every Sunday morning and Wednesday night, for the sake of Marice and his sons, and because his daddy went only to tent revivals and brush arbors to swear off devil whiskey. He would not listen to preaching of Jesus' love or any other from a criminal killer and escape artist.

"No," Gary Lee Stringer said. "I am talking about the here of this life. I do not care less for the next than yourself." That is the truth of it, Eldon thought, relaxing, wanting him to go on. "It is here what we have did. It is our loved ones, my lovely wife Linda Jean Stringer who comes of fine, high-type people of Soso, Mississippi, my darling daughter Darlinda, *here*," he said, his voice coming up. Eldon worried Fike McCain would sneak close, listen. "*Here!*" Gary Lee Stringer repeated, "in this very minute where we are, we are loving them. It is our misery to have to hate ourselves for all we have did, because we are men with something makes us ashamed."

"I ain't hating myself," Eldon said. He hoped he spoke the truth as he said it, wanted to be told it was really so.

"Ask your heart," Gary Lee Stringer said. They did not speak for a while. It was a time that did not pass, like when shouting Brother John Barnes stopped his mouth long enough to pass his eyes over the congregation to choose someone to lead prayer, when Eldon prayed to himself that he not be chosen to stand and witness.

"I am trying," Eldon said. And he knew it for a lie. He hated. He hated his daddy for being a pulpwood cutter for Masonite, trash. He hated being small and lean all his life. He hated his wife's uncle, and he hated living in a trailer house on a paid-up lot, hated what he had to be because he was who and what he was.

"Our hearts' truth is all what matters," Gary Lee Stringer said. "I seen killing and been a killer. I growed mean in hating. I robbed and used dope sometimes when I could not stand it no more. I had filth done on my skin with needles." He passed his large hands over the blue-black tattoos on his arms. "I would go on killing to the end except for the onliest thing of finding I love my wife and daughter in the true heart of my heart. I am talking about staying alive so I can still love something, so's the hurt you feel for what you have did is worth the feeling of it."

"I can appreciate it," Eldon said.

"The reason for my mood," Gary Lee Stringer said, "is I was just visiting my wife and darling daughter. The love of them has brung back my misery to me. The worst of it is knowing it is all over for me now. I will not rob and kill no more, but I won't see neither one of them again in this life. They have got me now."

He stood up close to the door of the cell, his face almost touching the bars. His eyes held Eldon's. His eyes were small and deep-set, bright with the hot truth he spoke. The skin of his face glowed in the hard light, flushed, gleaming, as if he burned inside with a fire hotter and hotter. His huge body threw a great black shadow back onto the floor of the cell. The white of his tee-shirt stood out starkly against the blue-black tattoos on his arms. His hands clutched the bars like he would squeeze them to powder.

"You always ex-caped before," Eldon said.

"Oh!" Gary Lee Stringer said, and he laughed, loud, like it was the biggest joke of all. "Don't you see? I am all done now. I won't rob nor kill and ex-cape no more. It's why I let them state police catch me so easy. I have truly looked in my heart. I found my love for my wife and darling daughter. The hurt of it is too much for me this time. I am all done. It is a hard way to go." Eldon did not want to believe it.

"I feel the exact same way myself," Eldon said. "Except it's the exact opposite. It's about all I never done in my life. You have robbed and murdered police and others," he said. Gary Lee Stringer raised and lowered his head, once, accepting the fact of it. "You are famous as a criminal. I seen you in the newspaper. I been seeing your picture in the newspaper. I been seeing your picture in the jail office."

"I do not deny it."

"Me," Eldon said, "I never did nothing I wanted to. It is the same with me except it's I never did nothing. I love my wife Marice and my boys and all, like you, but what hurts me is nothing done at all that is big or fine. I was a MP once in the army."

He wanted to tell him the particulars of it, that as a boy he was small and scared, that his people were trash, that he did not play football, that his wife Marice married him because he looked nice in his MP uniform, that he would be afraid not to witness for Jesus if Brother John Barnes ever called out his name, that he wanted a ranch-style house and to be sheriff and not just deputy because he married the sheriff's niece.

But the particulars would not come to words worth the saying. It was all little and mean. It hurt the way Gary Lee Stringer said it hurt him, because he loved something. It hurt never doing anything enough to match up with how much he loved.

"I accept it's too late for me now," Gary Lee Stringer said.

Eldon said, "What'd you do if you ex-caped from me here?" He looked into his eyes, and they looked at each other, and Eldon knew they would speak only truly to each other.

"Run to my lovely wife Linda Jean and my beloved darling daughter Darlinda. They are near Soso, with their people."

"Then what?"

"Away," Gary Lee Stringer said. "Where I am not famous. Me and them. We would go off, and no police nor newspaper ever find us again. I am speaking truly to you."

"I know it," Eldon said. He got up from his chair, laid the shotgun on the seat, stepped close to the bars so they could whisper.

"You dast not do it," Gary Lee Stringer said.

"I dast," Eldon said.

"They will carry *you* to Parchman for it."

"We will figure a lie for it. How I opened the cell to give you exercise, or better how you got sick and I opened up to see what was wrong and you run out too quick for me. I would have did something big," Eldon said. He touched the keyring tucked behind his cartridge belt. "They will believe me," he said. They would believe him because they would not believe he could do it. Because they could never believe he would do something. He took the keys from his belt.

"There's the colored," Gary Lee Stringer said.

"I will send him off," Eldon said. He had forgotten Fike, but Fike McCain would not stop him. Fike was like himself, Eldon thought. Fike was a nigger, and nobody would believe either of them doing anything for which a man could be famous. He was like Fike McCain, nobody expecting him to be anything but what he was.

"One more chance in my life," Gary Lee Stringer was saying, "I will disappear with my loved ones."

"I am giving you a chance because it is more for me than you," Eldon said. "Before it is too late for me to do a thing bigger than anything before or after."

Fike was in the jail office, dozing or pretending to doze in the sheriff's swivel chair. Had he been listening all the time? "Wake to hell up," Eldon said. "Get out and find me something to eat," he said. "I got to work double duty day *and* night, the county can afford me a snack."

Fike woke, if he was not pretending to wake, fluttering his eyelids open, twitching his mouth, blinking, yawning, showing his teeth and pink tongue. The whites of his eyes were yellowed. He licked his lips, pulled at his nose with his fingers. "Will you wake the hell up and do what I'm telling you?" Eldon said. He had left the shotgun on the chair outside the cell—what if Gary Lee Stringer was lying, just doing another famous escape? What if he was able to stretch between the bars, get the shotgun? Eldon shivered. He was doing a big thing. They had both spoken the truth of their hearts. "Damn you!" he said to Fike.

"Been sleeping," Fike said.

"Get out and find me something to eat. Now."

"Can't no place be open so late," Fike said. He looked at the wall clock, back at Eldon.

"Get your black ass out of this jail!" Eldon said. He grabbed him by the front of his shirt, stood him up. "Walk to the damn truckstop if you have to. Go to your own house or what-all, you get out of here now!" He shook the turnkey the way Marice shook his boys when they sassed her, the way schoolteachers shook Eldon when he was a boy, pushed and pulled at him. Fike's head rocked back and forth like it floated. Gary Lee Stringer could be touching the shotgun with his fingertips, stretching harder for a hold on the barrel or the trigger-guard.

"Leave me be," Fike said, and Eldon stopped.

"Please go out of here," he whispered, afraid his voice would break, that he might cry. How did men rob and kill and escape from prisons? How did anyone take someone's shoes and stomp their feet bloody? He did not think he could do anything big, ever. He would never be able to do anything. "Please?" he said.

"What you doing, Eldon Sistrunk?" Fike said. Eldon let go of his shirt. He could not think of anything to say. If Gary Lee Stringer had the shotgun now, Eldon still had his pistol. What if Sheriff Boyd showed up to check on him? What if his house trailer got on fire and Marice and his sons burned up. What if a tornado came and blew the trailer to pieces? What if Brother John Barnes called on him to lead prayer and his tongue stopped in his mouth? What if Marice's uncle was not elected sheriff next election? He could not look Fike McCain in the eye.

"Nothing," Eldon said. "Please," he said, "you got to." If Fike refused to go he knew he would not be able to force him. He would not be able to face Gary Lee Stringer, tell him he failed. He would not want to know the truth of anything ever again.

Fike left, mumbling. "Ain't no food place even open unless it gets six o'clock, and *you* knows it. Find nothing to feed nobody." He walked slowly, his shoes making no sound on the floor.

"Please," Eldon said.

"I need to do some sleeping here sometime," Fike said as he went out the front door.

The shotgun was still on the chair where he left it. "You truly do mean it," Gary Lee Stringer said. Eldon picked up the shotgun and unlocked the cell door.

"You got to run while it's still dark. You got to run and stay hid all through the daylight. I can't help no more after this. I am shut of it now. I am all through after doing this one thing."

"I will do it," Gary Lee Stringer said, leading the way out to the office, the jail's front door. "I have ex-caped before, I know the ways of it. I will get to my people at Soso."

"It will be in the newspaper again how you ex-caped once more," Eldon said as they stepped outside. It was still dark, but the feel of it was close to dawnlight. There would be a blurred touch of light in the edge of the dark soon, the birds begin their noise, the swish of traffic starting up on I-35 for the day, cars starting in Purvis.

"I will stop being famous when I get away," Gary Lee Stringer said.

"I *knowed* you doing something!" Fike McCain said. He had not gone away, only outside, up close behind them like he had never left in his sneaking nigger way. "You *doing* something!" Fike said. Eldon could make out the yellow-whites of his eyes, the grizzly grey of his raggy nap, shaking his head like he had come on a mess he would be made to clean up, clucking with his tongue.

"Run," Eldon said. Gary Lee Stringer started across the lawn, visible against the sky as light began to leak into the darkness. He did not run fast or well. He did not dash like a man who was a football player once. He did not run like he knew how to escape jails. He was a big fat man more hopping than running, a fat man with sore feet.

It was not like deciding, not changing his mind. This knowing was so deep Eldon only in that moment discovered it. There was no lie in it, had been no lying. It was greater than anything ever before in his life, ever after. It was the truth of his life, and the proving it all out in a great thing done. It was the sum and total of all his life, all he had not done to be famous or other than he was, coming now to an act that was larger than words. It was hurt made worse by wanting to love something, the discovery of more misery than ever before because he only discovered it as he acted.

He shot Gary Lee Stringer with the riot gun before he reached the edge of the lawn. Eldon fired once, the butt plate kicking into his shoulder, Gary Lee Stringer falling like he had stumbled over his own feet, down and lying still before the echo of the blast was clear of Eldon's ears. He thought he heard Fike Mc-Cain screech.

Fike ran to the fallen man, then stopped short of him, bent at the waist to see better, straightened up and stepped back quickly, as if the huge man lying there might reach out for him. Eldon lowered the shotgun, then put it on his shoulder, like marching in a military parade. When the light came full, he would have to find where the shell case ejected into the grass. He walked up to Fike.

"Dead as dead," Fike said, his voice high, keening. It was already light enough to see the wound centered in Gary Lee Stringer's back, the stain spreading in the white tee-shirt. "Deadest dead," Fike moaned.

"Do not worry," Eldon told him. "We can easy figure a lie they will believe."

"Dead," was all Fike could say.

"Do not worry. They will maybe even put you in the newspaper with me. We might could start being famous, Fike," Eldon said.

The Cold

Butch, determined to wait out the cold, took a stool near the end of the bar, away from the cluster of regulars gathered where they could see the Motorola TV. His back was only two feet from the front window. He could feel the cold seeping through the glass, hear the mean wind off Lake Michigan whipping the snow into drifts outside on Oakland Avenue. The frost was too thick on the inside of the window to see the storm in action.

Jeep Ervin came down from the far end of the bar to pour for him. "Come on, be sociable, Butcher," Ervin said. Jeep didn't change for the record weather. He kept the silver buttons on his red corduroy vest buttoned except for the bottom one. He wore a black Southern Colonel's string tie, and frilly burlesque garters on the sleeves of his white shirt to keep his French cuffs out of the wet. From where Butch sat, Jeep Ervin looked like a neat young man dressed for a party. Close up, Butch could see all the gray shooting through his hair, wrinkles, bags under his eyes behind his heavy hornrims.

"I still got a little pride," Butch said. Ervin marked the drink on Butch's tab. "Catch one yourself," Butch said.

"I'll take a cigar," Jeep said. He took a fifteen-cent Lark, unwrapped and lit it. "I'm surprised to see you out in this," he said.

"I wake up this morning," Butch said, "the apartment's cold as a tomb. I only got the one heavy blanket I took with me, you know. I call the super, he says the furnace went on the fritz late last night, he's working on it."

"Dream you were freezing to death," Ervin said. He checked the regulars at the other end of the bar, but they were all nursing their morning drinks, watching "NBC Today."

"No lie it's cold," Butch said. "I never dream though, you know? I swear, it's been since who laid the Chunk since I dreamed anything when I was sleeping. I let my troubles take care of themselves. You know, this very minute I'm supposed to be seeing some jerk in the family court downtown."

"Ex after you still?"

"Both barrels," Butch said. "I'm behind alimony and child support both. I figure, what can they squeeze when I'm all squeezed out, but, no, I'm supposed to meet this morning and explain with documentation." Ervin shook his head in sympathy. "She suspects I sold the car I said was in for repairs, I guess," Butch said.

"You did sell it?"

"What was I paying my rent with if I didn't? Next step I'll be over selling my blood with the hippies and winos."

"It's never that bad," Ervin said.

"I'd hang myself except I won't give anybody the satisfaction." Ervin laughed with him.

Somebody thumped a glass on the bartop at the other end of the room, and old Lois got control of her cough long enough to raise her glass over her blue hair and yell, "Jeep, honey, will you do me here again, please, sweet?" Butch watched Ervin go down the bar and serve his regulars a round.

Wallace and Len Wood were closest to him, on stools right in front of the cash register. Wallace's head drooped so far down between his sloped shoulders his chin all but dipped in his drink. Len Wood was in his usual trance, staring without blinking at his reflection in the backbar mirror, like he was trying to figure out which one was really him. Old Lois was a few stools down from them, to see the TV better, because Dinah Shore was next, her favorite. Her lighter, cigarette case, and compact were lined up on the bar in front of her. During commercials, when she wasn't lighting another Pall Mall, she opened her compact and fixed her face with her lipstick or puff. Every few minutes she got hacking hard enough to almost fall off her stool, regular as the Climatrol thermostat cutting in to keep the bar warm.

Hilton sat at the table-for-ladies, feet up on the table next to his glass. Butch had never seen him sit with his feet on the floor, like his center of balance was off a few degrees. Hilton talked back to the TV, grumbling into the beard he'd grown to cover his weak jaw and the chronic acne around his mouth. Little Philly Kolinski, laid off again from Rambler, sat next to Hilton, his best bet to cadge drinks, because Hilton always had plenty of pocket money.

"NBC Today" ran special coverage of the big storm. They brought in a network weatherman who showed maps of the huge cold-air mass spreading out from Canada all the way across Iowa, Illinois, and Indiana, lapping east over Ohio and Pennsylvania, into New York. They had on-the-spot film of trucks and cars abandoned on the toll roads, photographed from a helicopter. From Ohio, they covered the progress of some big plows cutting through to rescue families stranded in farmhouses, running out of food and fuel oil. They had a report from a man standing between two-story snowdrifts in Buffalo. Then they interviewed some government men and some men from oil and natural-gas companies explaining how supplies were running out and it all was going to cost more.

Then Hilton and Lois got into it over Dinah Shore. Hilton insisted Dinah was part Negro. You could see it in her goddamn lips and nose, goddamnit, he said. Lois said that was tacky talk she didn't believe for a minute.

"Sweet Jesus have mercy," Butch said. They all looked at him for a second, turned back to the TV when he didn't say anything more. Ervin came back to pour him another. "How in hell you keep from going bats with them around all the time?" Butch said.

"You're a pessimist," Jeep said.

"I'm a realist." Ervin went away. Dinah was answering audience questions. Butch got off his stool and faced the front window. The glass only a few inches from his face, the cold air passing into the barroom was like a wall he could step through if he

wanted to. He shut out the sound of Dinah on the TV, listened
to the whipping wind. It was only a whisper until he concen-
trated. Then he heard it whistle and roar, shriek through Oakland Avenue on the other side of the glass. The frost on the inside of the pane was like a coat of white paint.

Butch made a fist and rubbed a circle in the frost with the heel
of his hand. The air was all snow, the movement of the snow in
the wind only visible when he picked out a spot and stared at it.
He could barely make out the darker shapes of buildings across
the street, George Webb's Hamburger Parlor, Kalt's Bar, the
Fred Miller Theater. He couldn't make out East Side Federal or
Fran's Pizzeria or Plotkin's Deli. The intersection of Oakland
and Locust had disappeared behind the blowing snow. Oakland
Avenue was drifting full, drifts swelling up above the level of the
sidewalks. Parked cars were just mounds of snow at the curb
now. There was nothing outside but the snow and wind now, the
storm. His cleared circle clouded over.

For the hell of it, he made a fist again, pressed it to the window
until the heat of his body thawed a shape like a baby's footprint.
He added five tiny toes with the tip of his finger. The cold glass
numbed his fingertip. He made another baby's footprint, then
another and another. It looked like a pygmy had started to walk
the front window of Ervin's Bar.

"Hey, that's cute," Wallace said. He got off his stool next to
Len Wood and came over to the window. "I never seen that before," he said. He made one of the footprints.

Now they were all watching from their end of the bar except
Lois who had her head down to choke off a series of coughs. She
coughed as loud as a man, the way a horse would cough before it
foundered. Wallace made a pair of pygmy feet with the toes
pointing up, and then another pair between them, toes pointing
down. He barely finished it, laughing so hard.

"That's looking real neat on my window when it dries," Ervin
said. Wallace was bent over laughing, holding his stomach.

"You pig son of a bitch," Butch said. Wallace leered at him as
he returned to his seat next to Len Wood. "Pig mind son of a
bitch," Butch said.

"Look who's calling names," Wallace said when he was up on his stool again.

"Old lonesome me," Butch said. "You never seen me molesting little girls on playgrounds," he said, which shut Wallace up. The truth was, Wallace was never convicted of molesting a child, he was only suspected once a few years back. Since, detectives always checked him out when a new case came up anywhere on the east side of Milwaukee.

"What the hell is it with you guys?" Ervin said, trying to stop it before it started. But Hilton decided to join in.

"Who the goddamn hell rattled your goddamn chain?" he said from his chair at the table-for-ladies. Philly Kolinski laughed it up, waving his empty glass where Hilton could see it.

"Hilton," Butch said, "how's come you cultivate on your face what's growing wild in your crotch?"

"Honey, sweet," old Lois said without looking away from the TV, "I can't hear my show."

"Deadbeats shouldn't call names," Hilton said, and, "Jeep, better collect his goddamn tab now if you ever want to see your money."

"Sure," Butch said, "I never inherited a tire store." He knew Hilton didn't inherit a tire store. He had married it. "I didn't marry a bitch with money so's I could retire at forty and soak my head until I croaked," Butch said. Len Wood raised his eyebrows at himself in the mirror, like he was listening, but never turned away from his reflection.

"At least my goddamn bitch of a wife doesn't send deputy sheriffs looking for me," Hilton said. Philly Kolinski cut his laughter down to a smile to see if this was going anywhere.

"Jeep," Butch said, "tell a certain runt Polack snot he's subject to get slapped if he keeps up laughing at me."

"Honey, I can't hear what they're saying!" Lois said, pointing at the Motorola on its shelf. Dinah was over. Now it was a game show where contestants bet on movie stars to answer questions for them.

Butch said, "Bitch you married's so smart she gives you ulcers stealing change from her purse. Too bad she's not smart enough to cross her legs every time you dry out long enough to look her wall-eyed."

"Goddamn," was all Hilton could say. It was known fact Hilton's wife was mean, and they had seven children, the last one less than a year ago. From time to time Hilton had to climb on the wagon to heal the ulcer he got from trouble with the wife he married because she inherited a tire store from her father. Hilton took his feet off the table-for-ladies and stood up.

"Now look," Jeep Ervin said. He held his dead cigar like it was a lead-filled billy he was going to put up next to somebody's skull.

"You *fuckers*! I can't *hear*!" Lois said, then started coughing hard. She scattered her compact, cigarette case, and lighter clutching at the bar for a handhold to keep her seat.

Butch put his hands up. "Hobo your way over," he said to Hilton, "I'll pay your way back."

"Goddamn, damn," Hilton said.

"Big tough Butch," Wallace said, hunching up on his stool like he was afraid something was going to be thrown at him. "Tough Butchie," he said, "I heard you went to talk to your kid and he threatened to clean your clock for you. You weren't too tough then, were you." Hilton said goddamn again, but didn't move toward him. Philly Kolinski hugged his empty glass to his chest with both hands.

"Goddamn," Hilton said. "I heard your goddamn daughter won't answer the phone when you call. Deadbeat Butch," he said, "owes every-damn-body in town. I heard you're thinking of going bankrupt to beat your goddamn bills." Len Wood was listening, but didn't look away from the backbar mirror. Lois was coughing again.

"Big deal Butch," Wallace said, "big dealer, what are you selling for a living these days, Butch? Bibles? Encyclopedias? Better get on welfare, Butch."

"You winos," Butch said. He still had his hands up, but he unfolded his fists.

"Look who's talking," Wallace said, "How many jobs you lost for being sober, Butch?"

"Owes his goddamn ass to Household Finance," Hilton said.

"Where you drinking when Jeep pulls your tab?" Wallace said. "The Rescue Mission down on Water Street?"

"Goddamn deputy sheriff can find you there too," Hilton said. "Put your damn ass out in the House of Correction for ninety days, then let's hear you talk so goddamn much."

"Rumheads," Butch said to them. He could have said some more, but he no longer felt like fighting anybody. He didn't think he could whip anybody in a fight now.

"Throw him out in the snow, Jeep," old Lois said. "He's the one making too much noise for anybody to watch television."

O'Hara the beat cop came in just then, and that put an end to it. The door banged open like the wind had done it, and O'Hara lurched in. Snow came in with him like a cloud he threw off as he walked. The cold came in with him like a tidal wave washing over them all, froze them in place like statues, stopped their voices. O'Hara had to put his shoulder to the door and bull it shut against the snow piling up in the entranceway to the bar. The blast of snow and subzero air was like a burst of light, fading slowly after the door was closed and Ervin's Climatrol unit cut in with new heat. O'Hara stood in the middle of the room like a snowman.

"I'm *cold*," they heard him whisper. They had to lean toward him to hear. "Oh, it is so fantastically, spectacularly cold, Jeep," O'Hara said, his voice growing a little stronger. The earflaps of his winter uniform hat were tied under his chin, a civilian muffler over his face. Snow dropped off him to the floor, melted. The dark blue of his uniform began to show through his coating of snow. Philly Kolinski got up and helped him out of his wraps. "Oh," O'Hara said when he was free of his coat, "The most fantastic, stupendous, spectacular cold I seen thirty years walking a beat."

"You been stealing thirty years from the city," Butch said, but nobody heard him. O'Hara mounted a stool next to Wallace. Philly Kolinski joined him with his empty glass, since Jeep Ervin was pouring a round on the house to celebrate O'Hara's arrival. He poured O'Hara a double in a water tumbler, so he wouldn't spill his first drink with his shakes.

The drinking picked up with O'Hara there. The beat cop needed three quick doubles with a water chase before he was warm enough to lean back while Ervin poured the next round. Jeep gave them all four rounds on the house, and Butch went along with it, but stayed at his end of the bar. Then everyone bought a round by turns, except for Philly Kolinski, who didn't have a tab with Ervin. Butch put his round on the tab when his turn came up, but he stayed apart, pretended to be very interested in the noon report on WTMJ-TV.

WTMJ-TV had their own local special on the storm, running charts showing how the cold set new record lows for the past four days, how the Canadian air mass was stalled over the whole midwest and northeast. They reran tape from last night, Mayor Maier declaring the official snow emergency. Then they did remotes with the mini-cam, how deep the snow was downtown and on Lake Drive, way over on the west side, the freeways drifted shut, more snow predicted. They cut back live to the studio to read off public places closed, events canceled. They reported heart attacks caused by snow shoveling, and about a Polack woman froze to death drunk in an alley behind a tavern out on National Avenue, and a whole family of colored on Walnut Street without any heat or electric, how a church was setting up to take people in, keep them from freezing and starving.

"There you go, Butch," Jeep said, "in case your super don't get the furnace fixed."

"Butch don't mind niggers, only us winos," Wallace said, got a laugh from Hilton and Philly Kolinski. Butch wanted to do something about it, but didn't know what. He felt tired, and the drinks were getting to him now. He stepped away from the bar, like he was going to open the door for a look at the storm, got as far away from them as he could.

O'Hara was telling cop stories, how he had saved lives, delivered babies in kitchens and in the back seats of patrol cars, how the weather was a beat cop's worst enemy. He waved his hands as he talked, warmed up with the whiskey now. His leather cartridge belt creaked when he moved his arms. He was telling how once he cut down a suicide hanged himself in his coal bin in the basement. O'Hara's pistol stuck up and behind him in its holster. There was only a little leather strap with a snap held the gun in the holster.

Butch braced his back against the door. He could hear the wind clearly by the door, felt the cold oozing into the room around the frame. Four, maybe giant steps, he could reach O'Hara's stool. He could unsnap the leather strap, yank the gun out of the holster, be back by the door in a split second. He thought about it.

He could shoot them all. He'd shoot O'Hara first, just in case he thought he was still a real policeman and should try to stop him. Then he'd shoot Hilton, and then Wallace, and then Kolinski. He would shoot Len Wood before he ever looked away from the mirror. He'd shoot old Lois last, because she'd be stuck there, coughing, if she tried to run or call for help. He didn't know if he'd shoot Ervin. He couldn't remember if a pistol had five or six bullets. He didn't know what he'd do if he ran out of bullets and somebody was still alive. Or if he missed once or twice. He'd have to step real close to be sure not to miss.

"Butcher boy," Jeep said, "this one's on Len." Butch went back to his stool and drank the round on Len Wood. He noticed his hands weren't shaking. He was not nervous at all. He wondered if what he'd been thinking was just stupid. It surprised him he didn't feel the least bit foolish or nervous thinking thoughts like that.

The drinking slowed in the afternoon. The soaps came on the Motorola. Old Lois made a quick trip to the ladies', touched up her pancake, rouge, lipstick, and eye-liner, lit a fresh Pall Mall, turned around on her stool with a fresh drink to concentrate on "As the World Turns." Ervin lit a new Corona Lark and quit keeping track of who paid for what. When somebody was empty, he poured.

Len Wood showed his drinks some, blinking a lot at himself in the backbar mirror, raising and lowering his eyebrows like he was thinking amazing thoughts. Hilton was back at the table-for-ladies, feet up and crossed, grunting once in a while about the goddamn soap operas and the goddamn weather. Philly Kolinski stuck at the bar since Ervin was no longer taking money or marking tabs. O'Hara settled in for the duration, his fat behind spread out over the stool, leather creaking, cuffs and come-along chain tinkling like wind ornaments when he shifted his weight to give his piles a break.

Butch stayed at his end of the bar. He drank when Jeep poured, felt the whiskey put him into that place where nothing particular came to him. He didn't think about his ex, or his son or daughter, the finance company collectors out to garnishee wages he wasn't earning any more, sheriff's deputies with war-rants for him. He remembered what he had been thinking be-fore, and he'd catch himself staring at O'Hara's cartridge belt, the cross-hatched butt of his .38 police special jutting up and out behind him in its holster. He listened to the wind out on Oak-land Avenue, felt the constant flow of cold through the thickly frosted pane of glass at his back. He tried to imagine the snow blowing in the air outside, the drifts growing, but all he could think of was white, the whiteness everywhere. He couldn't imag-ine plain, real snow, couldn't bring up a memory of snowstorms when he was a kid. He never found himself remembering the past much.

WTMJ-TV broke in twice with special weather briefs. Once, the temperature had just set another record low for this date in history. The second time was just repeats of all the events can-celed, road-hazard warnings, places closed until further notice.

Butch stopped drinking when he couldn't focus his eyes to make out the time on the Budweiser clock suspended on a fake chain over Len Wood's nodding head. He could hear the TV, see the screen, but the colors blurred and ran. He couldn't make himself listen long enough to tell what was on. He noticed sud-denly how very quiet it was in Ervin's Bar. "No more," he said thinking to do something about it. Ervin came down to his end of the bar with the bottle.

"I'm cutting myself off," Butch said. "This is no way for a white man to live."

"Just don't be starting trouble again, okay, Butch?" Jeep said.

"I thought you wanted a refill," he said and went away when Butch didn't answer him.

Butch turned on his stool to face the front window. It was dark outside now. The cold came from the window, touched his face like a clean Lake Michigan breeze. He heard the wind singing in the street. When he turned back to look at the barroom he wasn't sure how long he'd been just sitting, feeling the cold, hearing the wind. For a second he thought the room might be empty, as if he'd passed out without dreaming, come to be locked in alone after closing time. But they were all there.

Lois was still facing the TV, but her head was down on her chest. He couldn't tell if it was her wheezing or Hilton's snoring he heard. Hilton had passed out with his feet up. Philly Kolinski had gone back to sit next to him, asleep with his chin on his hands on the table. Asleep, he looked even younger, like a baby sleeping. Wallace had passed out on his stool too, head sunk between his shoulders. Len Wood still stared at himself, but his eyes were almost closed. His expression was puzzled, like he'd come all the way through that concentration to meet his original question, surprised to recognize it. O'Hara's cheek was pressed flat on the bartop. His eyeglasses had come off. He didn't know where Ervin was until he heard water running in the men's.

Butch got off his stool and moved up behind O'Hara. He thought he'd take O'Hara's glasses, fold them away safely to one side on the bar. He didn't feel his drinks at all. Nobody seemed to see or hear him. Then he reached out and unsnapped the strap that held O'Hara's pistol in its holster.

He held his breath a beat, then took hold of the pistol and lifted it up and out of the holster, stood there holding the pistol a moment. He heard Ervin shut off the water in the men's. Now he held the pistol in both hands. It was heavier than he thought it would be. The cross-hatching on the grips felt sharp against his hand, and the barrel and cylinder felt very cool and hard against the skin of his other hand. The empty holster looked funny on O'Hara's belt. He unbuttoned his shirt and slipped the gun in next to his ribs, buttoned his shirt, covered it and held it in place with his arm.

"Ghost who walks," Ervin said when he came out of the men's. "Wake up and die right." He reached up and turned off the TV. "I'll fix us some instant," he said to Butch.

"Nature's calling," Butch said, and went into the men's. It was much colder than out in the barroom. He went into the stall and locked the door behind him.

He stood in the stall for a minute, then caught himself reading the writing on the walls. Ervin ought to paint that over, Butch thought, and then he felt stupid, holding O'Hara's gun next to his ribs with his arm. He unbuttoned his shirt and took it out carefully, afraid he might somehow snag the trigger on a button, that it might go off, blow a hole in the stall. He was suddenly afraid it would go off accidentally, shoot him in the hip or thigh. The stall area was too small to stand in with the gun.

Holding the pistol by the grips in one hand, he unlocked the stall door and stepped out by the sink, saw himself in the sink mirror, holding the gun. It felt especially cold in the men's because the air was so damp.

He took hold of the pistol correctly, lifted it all the way up, put the muzzle against his ear, careful not to press hard because it felt cold and sharp up against his ear. He posed that way for himself in the mirror. He couldn't keep from smiling at himself. He looked like a man in a cartoon saying goodbye to the cruel world. He took the gun away from his head.

Then he put the muzzle in his mouth, touched his lips to the barrel, careful not to let it touch the inside of his mouth. Even though he didn't touch it with his tongue, it was like he could taste it. The smell of it was oily, strong. The taste was like sucking a penny. He looked at himself in the mirror, with the pistol pointed into his mouth, holding it correctly with his trigger finger on the trigger. It didn't look funny at all.

"Hogs eat you?" Ervin hollered, banged on the door to the men's. Butch opened his mouth wider, took the gun away, not touching the inside of his mouth with it, careful not to bump his arm or the gun against the sink. It made him shiver, all the way through himself, as he thought how Ervin's yelling and banging on the door might have caused him to pull the trigger. It was so cold in the men's. It made him shiver to think Jeep Ervin might have opened the door to the men's and seen him that way with the gun. He placed the pistol on the bottom of the trash basket, covered it with paper towels from the dispenser.

"I thought maybe you passed out on the commode," Jeep said when Butch came out. He had a cup of Sanka waiting for him at the far end of the bar. Everyone else was still asleep. Lois and Hilton snored hard. Philly Kolinski twitched and whimpered like a dog chasing dream rabbits. Len Wood's face was all the way down on his arms at last. The indirect fluorescents reflected off the perfect circle of his bald crown. Wallace had spilled his drink, lay now with his face in the pool on the bartop. O'Hara had not moved. Butch picked up his glasses, folded them, set them far enough away to be safe. The holster on his belt just looked empty.

"I got to go, Jeep," Butch said, started for the door.

"Are you out of your wig, Butch?" he said. "Take a look once. You'll freeze your wazoo before you hit the corner." Butch went to the window, rubbed a spot clean. "Man, we'll be here all night unless the paddy wagon comes for O'Hara. Pull up a stool and drink your coffee."

The streetlight gave him a view, but all he saw was the air filled with snow, the total white of the drifted snow cover. The cold seemed to slip faster through the window pane, and he could hear the cracking of the winds as if it was right there inside with him. He shivered again. "The heat's still out in your apartment for all you know," Jeep said.

Butch turned back to him, looked at him, the sleeping regulars, O'Hara's empty holster. "I ain't sticking around here," he said.

"Get serious—" Jeep Ervin started to say, but Butch was at the door before he could finish. He yanked the door open, stepped outside, closed it behind him. "Your coat!" Ervin was shouting as Butch closed the door behind him.

He ran, not feeling anything at first, blinded by the sudden darkness, the wind that closed his eyes. He ran far enough to be sure Ervin couldn't see him if he came out after him, where his voice wouldn't carry against the wind. He ran blind into the force of the wind that was like a wall slowly falling onto him. He felt the wind tear at his ears and hair and hands. The drifts he ran through sucked at his feet.

He only felt the cold for an instant. He stopped running. He was somewhere in the snow, drifts up to his knees, some of them twisting up waist-high around him. He shielded his eyes with his hands, tried to slit his eyelids open to see where he was. There were some spots of light, streetlamps. They danced and shimmered with the shifts in the wind. There was nothing but the wind slashing at him, the drifts he stood in, the dark broken with trembling spots of light.

Then he was cold, so cold he wanted to scream—*cold*—cold everywhere on him, like new skin, like needles sticking him, something cold expanding inside him to join up with the wind. He felt flakes of snow like points of cold slamming, bouncing against his cold, hard skin. He thought of his coat and scarf and gloves left at Ervin's. The thought was too cold to make into words.

Then it passed. He went numb. Butch felt he had become part of this great cold, joined it with all of himself, and it could not hurt him. The noise of the wind didn't sound so loud now. His hands and arms and legs felt strong again. His breathing was easier. He felt he could talk or laugh, be heard above the roar of the storm. He had nothing he wanted to say. He didn't feel foolish or wrong. He didn't think of anything.

He started walking. He skirted the streetlamps, walked without lifting his feet so he could plow the snow aside as he moved ahead. He kept his head down, leaned into the wind. He didn't need to see where he was going. Even moving slowly, the footing was slippery, and he stumbled often to his knees, pushed back up, kept on moving. He began to feel comfortable, as if he was getting warm in the work of walking in the storm. He knew he might run into something, take a real fall he couldn't get up from, but he had no fear of it.

He slipped, regained his balance, slipped, fell, got up, slipped again, fell, got up, moved. He fell, fell again trying to get up, got up more carefully. Butch kept walking, moving, pushing on into the cold.

Getting Serious

When Captain Guy Roland of the Army Air Corps came home from the war, he drove his Lincoln Zephyr coupé right up to the edge of the bluff above Silver Lake, and blew the horn again and again to tell the world he was back. He leaned on it, long blasts that echoed out over Silver Lake, rolled through the pine trees, stopped us all where we stood, like an air-raid siren.

"What the goddamn hell!" my father said.

My mother ceased priming the kitchen pump with lake water, the pitcher in one hand, the other resting on the pump handle. "I think the Roland boy is back," she said, turning to see through the screened window.

"Where are you going?" my father said to me.

"I want to see."

"Let him go," my mother said.

"Far be it from me to insist on a damn thing," I heard my father say before the screen door slapped shut behind me.

Captain Guy Roland honked the horn of his Lincoln Zephyr, and his parents closed the bar and restaurant of the Silvercryst Resort and came outside. People came out of the bar and restaurant carrying glasses and bottles. Somebody gave him a bottle of beer he waved and pointed with while he dug things out of his duffel with his free hand. Everyone shook hands with everyone else.

The sun came through the swaying tops of the tall Norway pines, dappling us where we stood on the bluff above the lake. A light breeze rose off the water, stirring the surface of Silver Lake to glisten in the sun like chips of diamond or glass, lighting Captain Guy Roland's return. Mrs. Peaches Roland kissed her son on his cheek, his ear, his neck, keeping her cigarette away from his face. She carried a frosted Collins glass in her other hand. She said, "Baby, baby," to her son and kissed him again. I could see lipstick she left on his neck and jaw. He shook hands with everyone while his mother kissed him.

Mr. Roland shook hands with his son, shook hands with all the people who had come from the bar and dining room, then stepped back to some shade and smiled, squinting at it all, twirling the melting ice in the bottom of the glass he carried with him from the bar. Captain Guy Roland shook my hand.

"Our summerhouse is right next door to your resort," I said. I think he said that was keen, or swell, something like that, and then he was being kissed again by his mother and shaking hands with more people. The sun dappled us, the breeze swayed the tops of the Norway pines, shook the varicolored heads of the zinnias and marigolds and hollyhocks Mrs. Peaches Roland cultivated in tiered rockgardens on the slope below the bluff. The wind on Silver Lake shot the sun back up to us like the scraps of tinfoil that I saved to aid the war effort.

Captain Guy Roland gave his mother a ring in a wooden box. The ring was silver, set with pale stones, the box a dark, reddish wood, lined with purple silk. "That comes from Manila," he said. "Diamonds go there for a fraction what they're worth."

"Baby," Mrs. Peaches Roland said, kissing him with cigarette smoke coming out of her mouth. She carried the open box around for everyone to see, tried to make it sparkle by turning it to the light, clutching the box and her leather cigarette case and her empty Collins glass in her frail hands.

He gave his father a short Japanese sword. There were braided cords with tassels tied to the lacquered scabbard, and Guy showed us how the haft opened to reveal a piece of sheer rice-paper, spidery calligraphy. "You commit harakiri with it," he said. Prayers to your ancestors were written on the rice-paper to get you to heaven after you stabbed yourself.

"Wicked," Mr. Roland said when he unsheathed the sword

and put the ball of his thumb to its edge. The cigarette in his mouth made him squint and cough while he handled his son's gift.

"You hang that up over the fireplace," Guy said. He gave me a Japanese army forage cap and a wad of occupation money that also came from the Philippines. "In Manila you could buy a hot time with that," he told me. I stayed there and watched until Mr. and Mrs. Roland opened up the bar again and everyone went back inside the Silvercryst Resort.

These are not *living* details for me. Rather, after thirty years, it is a kind of tableau, a group of people frozen in my memory like statues, like a memorial to the people, the place, the world war. I can look at it whenever I wish, but it does not *live* for me.

We are set in place on the lawn next to the huge Lincoln Zephyr, outside the Silvercryst Resort bar and restaurant, dappled by the sun that penetrates the tops of the pine trees. We are frozen in place by the edge of the bluff above Silver Lake. On the slope descending to the beach, Mrs. Peaches Roland's bright flowers bloom. The water slaps at the dock and the moored boats, laps the sandy shore, lights our pageant with reflected sun that blares brilliant as an air-raid siren. I am part of it, this picture, yet outside it. It is my vision of the time and place of my beginning, but after thirty years it is no more than that.

Captain Guy Roland is the center of this picture. His hat, bent in a fifty-mission crush, is cocked back on his head, his blond pompadour ruffled as if by design. His captain's bars gleam, his pilot's wings a duller silver. On the left breast of his officer's dress-uniform jacket are the muted plots of color of his campaign ribbons and citations; the flat gold bars of his combat service track his sleeve. His uniform trousers, a faintest suggestion of pink, are sharply creased; the toes of his cordovan shoes glisten, spit-shined to the hardness of mirrors. *You can get diamonds for a fraction what they're worth*, he says, and *You hang that over the fireplace*, and *You can buy a hot time in Manila with that*.

My world, in this time of my beginning, is no more or less than my vision of it, and this picture is my vision, this time and place these people.

"Look," I said to my father when I came back to our summer home, "it's invasion money."

"That and a nickel gets you a cup of coffee," he said.

"He was a *pilot*, I think," I said.

"I flew a Spad at Fort Sill, Oklahoma," my father said. "You didn't know that, did you."

"You flew back and forth to Texas because you couldn't get whiskey in Oklahoma," my mother said.

"Another precinct heard from," he said.

"You should see that sword!"

"Any luck, some night in his cups the son of a bitch'll cut his throat with it and bleed to death," my father said.

"*Will* you stop!" my mother said.

"Not unless I'm asked nicely."

"He gave her a ring from Manila," I said.

"Know why they call her *Peaches*?" he said. "Ripe for the picking."

"Do you care at all what you say to him?" my mother said. My father did not answer her.

"In Manila you can spend this just like real money," I said.

"Get that nasty thing off your head," my mother said. "God only knows where it's been before now."

"And He ain't telling," my father said.

After their divorce, my father moved to Minneapolis and re-married. He wrote me regular letters I answered whenever I could not resist my mother's urging. He was, after all, she would say, still my father, even if he had abandoned us both. In my letters I told him yes, I was working hard and doing well in school, I was behaving myself, I was a help, not a hindrance, to my mother, I was enjoying the summer on Silver Lake. It was not lying, just something I had to say to please both my parents.

I remember it as my summer spent hanging about, lurking in some shade of pine tree or off to one corner of the beach, smoking cigarettes, watching, savoring my boredom and bitter envy.

In 1950 Guy Roland drove a custom Ford convertible. It was the summer I affected tee-shirts, my cigarettes rolled in one sleeve—hidden in the top of my sock when I had to go home to eat or sleep—wore Levi's slung low on my hips, black shoes with spade toes, my hair long on the sides and back, short on top. It was the summer season I gave over to hating myself for my boredom and resentment, detesting anything that chanced to come to my attention—except Guy Roland.

His father still ran the Silvercryst Resort, was still to be seen on the restaurant veranda, drink in hand, talking real estate with people who came to buy parcels of the lake frontage he had to sell. He was an immaculate man, his hair a spun white meringue, crisp shirts and casual slacks creased like knife blades. He wore two-tone brown-and-white shoes. He often stood on the bluff above the lake, jingling the change in his pocket, squinting against the glare of the sun off the water, as if counting the heads of vacationers who paid for beach privileges along with the cabins he rented. When he noticed me, he squinted a little harder, as if that was the closest to a smile of recognition he could muster. I would nod or shrug or blow cigarette smoke defiantly, flip butts into his wife's flowerbeds on the slope.

Mrs. Peaches Roland still came out late mornings to tend her zinnias and hollyhocks and daisies. Still light and colorful as the flowers she loved, she wore garden-party hats, the broad brims waving slowly in the lake breezes, tied under her chin with swaths of filmy gauze. She carried her cigarettes and lighter in the patch pockets of her pastel smocks, one hand free to carry a trowel. Eyes shaded by opaque aviator's sunglasses, she teetered as she stepped among the blossoms on platform shoes with open toes. The flaming reds of her lips, fingernails, and toenails always matched. When I slouched close enough, I heard the popular songs she hummed to herself, caught the wall of scent that surrounded her like a sweet cloud.

Guy Roland came and went all summer. I remember it as his perfect summer, the season I would have signed away my future to share the smallest part of—one week, a day, an afternoon.

Like the summer he came and went. He always had friends. From where I brooded, some shaded corner of the resort I do not recall, I heard the crunch of the Ford's whitewalls on the gravel parking lot. The convertible's radio carried through the pines, played all the way up so they could hear it through the wind whipping them as they drove—from wherever to wherever. He pulled his car right up on the grass and pine needles at the edge of the bluff, always honked the horn in some rhythm as his friends climbed out without opening the doors. *Watch the paint, watch the paint*! he would say. He and his friends would laugh.

He drove barefoot. He and his friends were barefooted, wearing swimming suits, carrying bath towels and beach blankets, a big portable radio, cigarettes, and bottles of suntan lotion, sunglasses, unbuttoned shirts with tails that hung down over their swimsuits.

The girls were always beautiful—long legs, skin tan-gold, hair pulled up off graceful necks, pouty lips, full breasts bound in halters or swim-tops. Some of the men wore sweatshirts with the sleeves cut off raggedly, faded Greek letters on their chests. His friends started down the slope to the beach while Guy went to the bar for their beer.

I put myself in his way whenever I could do it without awkwardness. If he saw me, he would nod or wink, or say hello, and I would nod, smile, wave my cigarette at him, make that do for the day.

"So what's the program plan?" Mr. Roland would say if he could catch Guy before he got away from the bar with paper cups and the cooler of beer.

"Busy, Popper, busy," Guy said to his father. "Hello there, Miss Peaches!" he would shout to his mother among the flowers as he passed her on the way to his friends. His mother waved, blew a kiss to his back as he disappeared down the slope. I followed no sooner than I had to.

Guy Roland and his friends spread their blankets on the sand, extended the radio's antenna to bring in the music of Chicago and Milwaukee, popped caps off bottles of beer, rubbed lotion into each other's shoulders. The beautiful tan-gold girls untied their halters, lay down on their stomachs to brown the whole of their broad glazed backs. I could get near enough to smell the tang of the oil. Guy Roland sat up on one elbow, squinting at the harsh sunlight reflected off Silver Lake. The breeze flipped his blond hair. He smoked cigarettes and drank beer, kept time to the radio music with one foot, the vision of a man in his perfect summer, a perfect life awaiting him in the distances not quite visible beyond the far shore of the lake.

They lay, soaking in the sun, seldom touching, never swimming, paying no attention to the children who dabbled in the shallows, the boats that docked and left—never noticing me, squatting at the base of the slope, souring my mouth with cigarettes, almost content with nothing more than my vision of them—static, impervious, unconcerned. It is a picture, but I am never in this one.

Guy Roland came and went, from Memorial Day through Labor Day, this summer I call the season of my rage at myself for being what I was without even the right to claim that I had made myself what I had become. His father ran the Silvercryst Resort and sold what remained of the lake frontage that he owned. Peaches Roland babied her flowers late mornings, drank away afternoons and evenings in the resort bar. What I hated most was my conviction that nothing would ever change.

"Where have you been so long?" my mother asked me when I returned.

"Nowhere. Down by the beach."

"I smell cigarette smoke."

"Cut it out," I said.

"You've been smoking!" she said. "What would your father say if I wrote and told him you smoke?"

"Come on, cut it out."

"I give up," my mother said to me. "You don't listen to me. When are you going to be serious about anything?"

"I'm serious," I said. I was.

The truce had been signed for two years by the time I came back from Korea. I was hospitalized a long time in Japan, a long time in Fitzsimmons Hospital in Denver, and a long time in outpatient rehabilitation at Fort Sheridan, Illinois, while I tried out my rebuilt knee in what they called *real-life situations*. They rebuilt my knee with steel and wires and plastic, and it worked fine. I only used a cane because I was afraid it might give way at any moment. They said that was psychological. I thought I could hear my rebuilt knee make a clicking noise when I walked, but that was psychological too. My mother was very nervous about it.

"You're being silly," I told her. "It's the strongest part of my body. It's like a spotweld, the last thing that's going to break."

"I'm sorry," she said, "I can't help worrying." She had not changed while I was away. She looked just a little older. She was really upset only when we happened to talk about my father, who had died suddenly in Minneapolis just before I came back from Japan.

"It's nice," I said. "Seriously, nothing's any different." She had not changed, except to look, naturally, a little older, and of course my father was dead, but he had gone out of my life years before.

It was night, so I picked my way slowly with my cane across the patches of moonlight breaking through the pine trees. I stopped to rest on the bluff, watched the moonlight ripple on the surface of Silver Lake. The lake stretched out below me, shimmering with the moon-haze that drifted over the pines above and behind me. Dock lights defined the far shore, and I could hear the same lapping of the water against the beach, the wind swish in the tops of the pines, the rustle of insects in the grass and ferns at my feet. I could hear the music of the jukebox in the bar of the Silvercryst Resort.

I knew what I would not find. Mr. Roland was also dead, my mother told me, a suicide. He shot himself about the time I was in Denver. She did not know the story. Business, perhaps, or his wife. He drove out on a dirt road, put the barrel of a pistol in his mouth, killed himself. Maybe it was his wife.

Peaches Roland had begun to need long stays at a downstate sanitarium, drying out. Now, my mother said, her mind was gone and she was committed forever to the sanitarium. "You ought to see how he's let her rockgarden go," my mother said.

Guy owned and operated the Silvercryst Resort, but he was no businessman, my mother said.

I expected at least a small crowd on a Friday night before Labor Day weekend, but the bar was empty except for Guy and a woman. The jukebox glowed, played loudly, and the fluorescents lit the back bar softly, but there were only the two of them, sitting on stools at the end of the bar as if they were customers, the bartender on a short break.

I smiled, put my weight on my cane, held my hand out to him. Guy Roland stared at me for a moment—the woman with him did not raise her head until we were introduced—then squinted, recognized me, smiled, took my hand.

"You don't have to wear your war suit," Guy said. "I'll serve you even if you're not of age. Hell, we're old folks, you and me."

"I'm old enough," I said, "just. I haven't had much chance to buy something that fits."

"Meet Sue," he said. The woman smiled at me as if I were going to take her picture. She was a good-looking woman. "This is my old buddy what's-his-name," Guy said to her, and "Sue is a personal guest here. I stress *personal*," he said, "because I hear rumors she favors men in uniform." She laughed and lowered her face to her drink—she drank bottled beer, liked to peel the labels off the bottles, pile the scraps on the bar. I said hello, and she laughed but never, I think, spoke to me all the time I sat talking with Guy.

She was fine-looking. I imagined her one of the girls who came and went with Guy through the summers before I went away. I could see her as one of those girls on the beach, gold-tan skin glossed with lotion, unfastening her swimsuit top to get the sun evenly across her back while she napped away the season's afternoons on a blanket, the portable radio playing music from Chicago and Milwaukee.

She was old enough to have been one of those girls, paled now because she spent her time indoors, wearing dangle earrings and chain bracelets that slid and rattled on her bare white arms as she picked at the label on her beer bottle. In the lulls of the lake breeze coming through the screened windows facing the bluff, her heavy scent reminded me of Mrs. Peaches Roland drying out forever in a downstate sanitarium.

"Drinks on the house!" Guy said. "You name it, you got it," he said, "just so I can get to it without moving, that is." Sue laughed and tinkled her bracelets. Guy stretched across the bar, pulled up a bottle, splashed a refill in his glass—he did not bother with ice and water or soda. He spoke clearly, weaved a little when he tried to stand or walk, but did not stumble or stagger. When Sue wanted another bottle of beer to tear at, she got up and went behind the bar for it herself. She looked fine walking, too, jewelry glinting and ringing, her skin very white under the fluorescents. Guy grunted, stretched far enough to find me a shotglass.

"I'm not used to taking it straight," I said, but he paid no attention.

"Happy happy," he said, and we all drank. He closed his eyes when he drank as if he needed to concentrate to get the full taste of it, touched his lips lightly with his forefinger after he swallowed, sighed like a man falling into a long deep sleep. "So what the hell's with the walking stick?" he said. I told Guy and Sue about the mortar shell that fell near me. "You're crapping me," he said.

He leaned close to me, squinted, as if the campaign ribbons I wore contained fine print. "Real?" he said. "This is a *real* Purple Heart?" he said, pointing.

"That's the Syngman Rhee Citation. This one's the Purple Heart."

"You got to be crapping, buddy," Guy said. He made me pull up my trouser leg, show him the swollen, pink-stitched seams. I told him how it was rebuilt with steel and wire and plastic, that I imagined at times I could hear it click when I walked.

When he stopped laughing he said, "Six bits in the PX and you go off and get yourself the *real* thing!" Then he told me how he spent his war at Pensacola, Florida, some kind of air-corps liaison with the navy's flight-training school. The work called for a captain, so they made him a captain. When Sue laughed, she was laughing to herself. His campaign ribbons had all come from the Pensacola Naval Air Station PX, bought the day he got his separation papers.

"Why the hell not? My folks got a bang out of it."

"You bought those souvenirs at the PX too?" I tried to see into the darkened dining room, see if a Japanese sword hung over the natural-stone fireplace.

"I could get all that crap I wanted from the swabbies passing through flight school. You forget that was a *big* war, son," he said.

We talked, and we drank from Guy's bottle; and when I was feeling the whiskey, I told him my father was dead. When he only nodded, I said, "I was sorry as hell to hear about your father."

"That's a whole long story itself," is all he said, drinking, pressing his finger to his lips to dry them. Sue kept the jukebox playing, reaching into his pocket for quarters whenever it stopped.

"I'm sorry about your mother."

"She just needed a rest," he said. "You can understand a person needing a rest. Like yourself," he said. And: "So what the hell you figuring on now?"

"Home and sleep it off. If I can keep from going over the bluff with this cane." Sue thought that was funny, laughed with us.

"Smartass," Guy Roland said, "I mean your damn life."

"College, I think," I said, and told him what the GI Bill plus my permanent disability pension came to every month. He squinted at college, like it was a book he tried to recall reading, then smiled as if remembering it was amusing, but not serious. He had tried college, a couple of those winters that hit so quickly after Labor Day, upstate in Wisconsin.

"Don't break your fanny on my property," he called to me as I went out the door, keeping my cane out carefully in front of me—I believed my knee was going to collapse somewhere in the dark.

"Hey," I said, looking back at them from the doorway, "Where's everybody? Is this Labor Day weekend or not?"

"He must think this is a business or something!" he whooped. "Close the screen door, you'll let mosquitoes in," he said, and got up to stretch for his bottle again.

My mother waited up for me. "What did you find to do all night?" she asked.

"Talking with Guy." I did not kiss her, did not want her to talk about the dangers of drinking so much when I could so easily fall and really hurt myself. "It's like a tomb at Silvercryst," I said to be saying something as I went toward the porch where I always slept at Silver Lake.

"He'll finish the ruin his father started," she said. "He takes no care at all."

"It's sad," I said, but my mother had no sympathy to spare for Guy Roland and his parents. I lay on my bed on the sleeping porch, waiting for the spinning whiskey to slow so I could sleep. When I could clear my mind I stayed awake a while to plan my life. I felt very good about it, as if my life was something I just discovered that I owned, mine to do with as I wished. I was pleased to discover that I was so mature.

I went to college and I got married. I studied nothing in particular in college, but I was graduated. The girl I married came from a very good Winnetka family. I learned the construction business from my father-in-law. I did not marry the boss's daughter and take over his business; I worked very hard, and the business was better for my work. First I lived in a fine home in Winnetka, near my wife's parents. After my children were born, I built a wonderful new home for us out in Skokie, where we lived close to wealthy Chicago doctors and lawyers and a few men who, like myself, were very serious about what they did for a living.

We built luxury condominium developments that sold as fast as we built them, and I had first a son, then a daughter, and a special wing on our wonderful home in Skokie where my mother lived with us the last two and a half years of her life. I had no trouble at all in my life, and even my marriage was as good as most marriages—most of the time.

When my mother died, in the late spring of 1965, I used that as an excuse to go up to Silver Lake. "We can all go," I told my wife. "The kids would love it. You might even like it. Mix pleasure with business," I said.

"That's your story," she said.

"I can't sell it out without being there," I said. "Those country real-estate boys will rob me blind."

"I'm *not* packing us all up and hauling all the way up there," she said.

"I have to go," I told my wife. "I can't handle it long distance."

"You do what you think you have to."

"I always have," I told her. "That's why I'm so good at it. Or didn't you notice?"

My wife and I never talked about our failing marriage, because it was too serious and depressing a topic and because, I suppose, we thought our failure would heal itself if we left it undisturbed long enough.

A lake, something in nature, does not change. The water level goes up or down a little from year to year, but as I stood on the bluff above Silver Lake, the moon still shimmered coldly on the surface, the breeze shushed in the tops of the pines above and behind me, the far shore was steady with dock lights. I did not see the fading paint on the summer home in the dark that first night, did not notice the pine needles banked up against the house by the winter, the remains of our pier heaved and broken by the winter ice; but inside, the walls held the musty damp of the closed winter that I remembered from opening the house each season after Memorial Day, years ago. Inside, everything was in place, clammy to the touch after several years undisturbed, but whole and unworn. The music still came through the air from the Silvercryst Resort, higher and stronger than ever, drowning out the lapping of the water at the beach below the bluff.

The resort was very crowded—the bar, the dining room, the new wing that held a second small bar and a sandwich shop and a souvenir counter. The music was a man in a tuxedo jacket and bowtie, playing a piano-bar. He had a machine he worked with a foot treadle. When people shouted requests from the dining room or the bar, or a woman at the piano-bar bent close to his ear to whisper a request, he riffled the keyboard, smiled, nodded that he knew the song. With his foot treadle he flashed a slide of the lyrics on a white screen mounted on the far wall. The projector was built into the piano-bar. The projector light also illuminated a nameplate on the piano-bar that said *Little Freddie Kay*.

The bartender was a man my age. The crowd kept him busy, but not too busy to take the drinks he was offered when someone ordered a round. He was a thin man with very black hair, long sideburns, a black moustache, a goatee so black it looked pasted on his chin. He wore a white shirt with ruffles, a red satin vest, frilly red garters on his sleeves to keep his cuffs out of the wet. He wore a colonel's string tie, trying for a western or 1890s idea in his costume. "Where's the boss?" I asked him. I had to speak loudly to be heard—Little Freddie Kay worked the projector treadle, and the crowd sang along with him. "On the Road to Mandalay." "K-K-K-Katy." "Down by the Riverside."

"Me myself and I," he said, grinning at me. He had very small and deep-set eyes, as black as his goatee, always lively, as if lit indirectly, like his backbar.

"Guy Roland?"

He grinned again. "He'll be along."

"You own this place now?"

"Since many moons back," he said, and went away from me in a hurry because they were calling for another round at the far end of the bar, insisting that he have a drink with them.

"You a friend of Guy's?" the new owner of the Silvercryst Resort stopped later to say. When he grinned, his white teeth were very white against the black of his moustache and goatee. I wanted to reach out and pull his goatee off, but his white pointed teeth were like a dog's when the dog snarls.

"I used to know him a long time back."

"Now Guy is a man can drink drink for drink with you," the new owner of the Silvercryst Resort said, "but he only puddle-jumps now," he said, and shook his head and changed his grin to a sad grin. Little Freddie Kay sang "Waltzing Matilda" and "Roll Me Over in the Clover," and the crowd roared along with him. I waited, wondering why I was not with my family in my wonderful home in Skokie, and thought about my father who left me when I was fourteen, my mother who had only recently died. From time to time I tried to see through the reflections in the thermal panes of the big picture window, see the opposite shore, but could not make anything out clearly. Little Freddie Kay and the crowd sang "There'll Be a Hot Time in the Old Town Tonight."

When Guy Roland came in they were all singing "Row, Row, Row Your Boat." I remembered his drinking, but he was only a puddle-jumper now. He sat among all the singers who were singing "Danny Boy" now, sat in the middle of the singers and big drinkers, as quiet as if he were absolutely alone in the room. He did not call out or wave for the bartender. He sat on his stool looking straight ahead at nothing, somewhere in the reflecting glass of the picture window that was supposed to frame the view of Silver Lake. He stared like a man who sees only what he is thinking about.

When the new owner of the Silvercryst Resort chanced to look his way, Guy raised one finger, made a dry kissing motion with his lips to order the beer he drank now that he was only a puddle-jumper. I waited before going over to speak to him, to get two things firm and clear for myself. One was that I could never again truly imagine the past. The other was that I would have no difficulty imagining the future.

I could no longer imagine Captain Guy Roland of the Army Air Corps returning from the world war. I remembered it clearly, had it as I would have a snapshot in an album, and I was in that picture, but it was just something I remembered. I could no longer imagine Guy Roland coming and going, coming and going in his custom convertible through the long summers of my own ripening season. I remember his sporty car, and the tan-gold skin of the girls, his friends with their cutoff Greek-letter sweatshirts, the smell of suntan lotion in the lake breeze, music on a portable radio, but it is just another picture.

There were many fine-looking women in the new Silvercryst Resort bar, types of the woman Sue who tore labels off bottles all one night in that same room, ten years before, but I could not imagine Guy Roland anywhere before that moment, watching him drink his beer slowly while Little Freddie Kay led the hoarse crowd in "Oh! Susannah."

What I got very clear for myself, watching him from my end of the bar before I went over and spoke, was that time and change are facts of life for all of us. Time and change are what we are talking about when we talk about the future, about what we want for ourselves in life. These are the facts of life.

He would have, I saw, the spun white meringue hair of his father—already the blond was shot with silvery streaks that caught highlights. He wore his hair longer, in the new fashion, slicked with dressing to hold it all in hard and perfect order. His face had thickened to hint of jowls and double chin—Guy would grow heavier with the years. His cheeks, the tip of his nose, were lightly flushed—the years, doubtless, when he had matched every drink. Years of cautious puddle-jumping would not bring back the fairness of his prime. His blue eyes were still bright, like the eyes of a child after weeping, but ten years clung to him like a sad chronicle laid down in sedimentary stone.

"It's my turn to buy a round," I said. He recognized me at once.

"I'm double damned," Guy Roland said. His handshake was still solid, his voice unbroken; it was like hearing a recording that holds its fidelity after years of storage. "Your money's no good here," he said, taking out a clip of bills.

"This puddle-jumper," the new owner said, "I seen the day he'd drink you drink for drink, make you beg mercy."

"A real authentic shit," Guy Roland said when he left us.

"Why'd you sell out?" I asked. He had an easy laugh that had been used too often and too easily to ever be able to mean anything is ever funny any more.

He said, "Six of one, half a dozen of the other. I took enough out that I'll never have to work a day in my life. My old man always told me I had no head for business," he said. "All I needed was a few seasons to prove it." I looked to the door, to be sure there was a path I could maneuver with my stiff knee—in case I wanted to get away in a hurry. "The sauce," he said, tipping his glass to show me the beer in the bottom. "I was bombed for years. The amazing thing is I lightened up once I cut this place loose. I go three, four weeks at a crack without touching hard stuff. Keep an eye on yourself," Guy said, squinting, laughing, nodding at my drink; "a man can end up like Miss Peaches before he knows he's halfway there."

"I'll stay alert," I said, meaning it.

He told me Mrs. Peaches Roland was still alive, still lived in the downstate sanitarium. I told him my mother was dead, that I had come up from Chicago to see about selling the summer home. "Sell, sell," Guy Roland told me. "All the lake frontage's gone. You can turn it over in a minute. Get smart. Get free of it while the getting's good."

I told him I would, deciding I would not. I told him I was married, about my wife and son and daughter in our wonderful home in Skokie, Illinois, about constructing condominiums that sold faster than my father-in-law and I could build them. He stared off at nothing as I talked, licked his lips, savored the beer he drank three or four weeks at a time before he jumped into another puddle of the hard stuff. He did not tell me he was not married, that he did nothing, because he did not have to. I could read him as clearly as if his life were projected for me on the screen by Little Freddie Kay, between the lines of song lyrics.

Before I left, I asked him, "Guy, do you remember that girl Sue?"

"The which?"

"Sue something. She used to hang in here with you. Years ago."

"Sue," he said, trying to see something in the empty air in front of his eyes. "Double damn me if I do," he said. Why should his memory have been any better than mine?

Another ten years passed, and things were very different. When my father-in-law died, there were problems with our construction business—he left less in it than I thought he would. The construction business went bad for everyone, and almost nobody could afford to buy condominiums. Then I could not get money from banks to build them any more. Still it was not so bad until my wife divorced me and took almost everything that was left. Then I was no longer in the construction business.

I did not live in the wonderful home in Skokie, and I did not see my former wife or my son or my daughter any more. I had to drive up to Silver Lake in the dead of winter to sell the summer home because I needed the money badly, in a hurry, because I had almost nothing left. Guy Roland had put me in touch with a real-estate agent named Harley Eagan who, Guy wrote, handled most of the lake frontage that was bought and sold on Silver Lake these days.

I was almost snowblind for a moment, my eyes running tears from the bitter wind, when I got inside the Silvercryst bar. I stomped my feet free of snow, brought the sting of feeling back into my toes, coughing on the sudden warm air. When I took off my coat it was like taking off the cold winter air, like the season had changed back suddenly to late spring. Harley Eagan and Guy and the new owner of Silvercryst and another man I did not know were waiting for me. I thought at first they had opened the resort especially for me.

"Check his ID card, members only," the fourth man said.

"Welcomewelcomewelcome!" the new owner said.

"There's my man!" said the man who was Harley Eagan the real-estate agent. I knew his voice from the telephone. "Give the man a glass," he said. "He's about to dry up and die from exposure.

"No havee membership card, no drinkie drinkie here," said the man I did not know.

"Lighten up, Major," Guy Roland said. "This man's a war hero. I saw the scars myself." It was some kind of club. I dried my eyes on my handkerchief and, shaking, drank whiskey with them to start warmth inside me. They were a club of sorts, meeting daily through the long winter at the resort bar to drink themselves through the long off-season. I think they were close to madness, together like that all winter long.

"I'll be wanting to see those scars," the major said. I never got his name. He was a retired army major, and they called him Major, and almost never listened to him or answered when he spoke. He wore his pepper-salt hair crewcut, and he drank more than any of the rest of them.

"Stuff a bar rag in his mouth," Guy Roland said to the new owner of the Silvercryst Resort.

"Shut your face, Major," the new owner said. "Don't mind the major. The major's a good man. He'll drink you under the table with your little tootsies turned up to the sky." The new owner had not changed. In the dead grey light of winter that came in the frosted windows, the stark black of his hair and moustache and goatee was more obviously dyed than I remembered. He had put off his vest and colonel's tie because he had no clientele in winter. His small eyes were still lively, and his pale hands never shook when he poured drinks or lit a cigarette with a lighter that flamed up high and made everyone laugh each time he lit it. "Flamethrower," he said, turning his head away and lighting it again. "Hey, Major, flamethrower!"

"A little pleasure mixed in won't hurt our business, mister," Harley Eagan said when I tried to talk to him about his selling the summer home quickly for me. "Put the next one on my chit, pal," he told the new owner. He reminded me of my ex-father-in-law, who was dead. My dead ex-father-in-law was not an alcoholic, but like Harley Eagan he smelled of aftershave and cologne and the lozenges that a successful alcoholic sucks to cover the drink on his breath. He dressed carefully, tweed jacket and vest, heavy gold cufflinks and tietack, thick digital wristwatch, big Masonic ring. He wore an old-fashioned hairpiece—when I got close I could see the delicate net pasted to his forehead, the artificial brown of the hairpiece marked off sharply from the washy grey of the hair above his ears, at the back of his head.

"I *need* to sell," I told him.

"Get too eager, mister, you'll take a beating. I know."

"Pay heed," the new owner said. "You're talking to the richest booze-hound in this and three counties. And a charter member of the Silver Lake Drunks, Incorporated," he said of Harley Eagan.

"You see me in what I'd call my element," Guy Roland said. Past fifty now, he was different, yet the very same. He was exactly as I would have imagined him, if I had bothered, over the years. His hair was now exactly his father's spun white. He wore it sculptor-cut over his ears, sprayed to hold a sweep low across his brow. He had gained a lot of weight, but covered it with a loose peasant smock—like his mother, Peaches Roland, used to wear to tend her flowers. He wore a bead choker, denim trousers, tan moccasins.

"How's your mother doing?"

"She goes on like time itself," he said.

"I thought you only jumped from puddle to puddle," I said.

"This is the puddle. Get it?" the new owner said.

"I'd go insane if I tried to dry out," Guy said.

"This puddle's so deep we grow gills just to keep breathing," the new owner said.

"I confess I never shed blood for our flag," the major was saying.

"Winters I lie low," Harley Eagan said, tapping his temple with his forefinger, as if there was a delicate mechanism there he might set right with the proper nudge. "It's spring I get hustling. I turn over lake property like a one-armed paperhanger. I'd be afraid to tell the tax man the commissions I rake in, mister," he said.

"Jesus wept," I said to nobody there.

"So," Guy Roland said, "how's it feel to get up in your old stomping grounds again?"

Through the frosted thermal windows the sky crept lower and darker with the snow it promised. I tried to see through to the lake, but had to imagine the sweep of the blowing snow over the ice, vehicle tracks, a few ice-fishing shanties, the exact line of the opposite shore hidden under the snow cover, the stark trees. The dining room was closed off, the piano-bar draped with a cloth—what happened to Little Freddie Kay? I wondered.

"I'll be damned if I'll try to stay sober through a winter here," Guy said.

"I could sell cheese boxes sitting on postage stamps if it had some lake frontage, come spring, mister," Harley Eagan said.

"Military life requires a special breed of man to stick it out," the major was saying.

"What if I next year locked myself in here alone and reduced the inventory all by my lonesome," the new owner of Silvercryst Resort said. "What'll you booze-hounds do for laughs then? Major, you'll go completely nuts, won't you!"

Jesus wept, I thought. I thought about all the people I had known in my life who were dead, and I thought of my ex-wife and my son and my daughter who were gone from me, and how when I saw them they would be so different, so changed they would be like new people I did not know. The people who were gone from me were like all the people who were dead.

I thought about all the summer homes on Silver Lake, closed up for winter, dark, empty, how the frozen lake was like the flat expanse of a cemetery, given up to cold and wind and snow. It was getting dark outside already. The four of them—five counting myself—were like last survivors, mourners huddling for the last warmth of the last fire, praying on our stools for the hope of springs and summers we have almost forgotten, that we remember only in the way feverish dreams are remembered. I closed my eyes, tried to forget everything about everything I ever knew. I must have said something, because Guy Roland heard me.

"Don't take life so serious," he told me. "It ain't even permanent." I opened my eyes, breathed very deeply, shook my head to be sure it was not the whiskey making me talk.

"Oh, it's serious," I said.

"No, it's not," he said, finishing his drink, setting the glass on the bar for a refill.

"I know better," I said.

"No, you don't," he said. He held up his fresh drink, squinted to see through the whiskey to the window, out the window into the winter dark.

I said, "Even if it's not, it used to be." He drank, puckered his lips, shook his head as he held the drink in his mouth, rolled it on his tongue. No. It was not. "At least for me it was, once," I said. He looked out the window, drank again, shook his head. No, not even for me. "Then what are we even talking about it for?" I said. He shrugged.

I left as quickly as I could. I settled the picture of them together there, half-mad, and I was in it, and not in it, and then I left. Thinking, I sat a long while in my car, letting the engine warm, the heater going. I thought about it all the way back to Chicago on the superhighway made treacherous by swirling snow and patches of ice. I could wait for spring to sell the summer home, a better market.

I thought about all the dead and living people I knew, and about the living people like Guy Roland, who were dead, and about all the living people who had gone from me, like the dead. I thought about all the living people I knew who were all going to die, when they died, or before they died.

I drove slowly so I would not worry about the road. I did not play the radio, tried not to read the green and silver signboards with the names of all the small Wisconsin towns, so I could think about all this, and about myself.

I tried to decide if I was living or dead. If I was living, would I wait to die to be dead, or if I was already dead, when had it happened? How long had I lived? These are serious questions. I do not ask them lightly, and I continue to work on the answers.